Are We There Yet?

Rach and Jules take to the open road

Rachael Weiss with Julie Adams

ALLEN&U

Allen & Unwin
83 Alexander Street
Crows Nest NSW 2065
Australia
Phone: (61 2) 8425 0100
Fax: (61 2) 9906 2218
Email: info@allenandunwin.com
Web: www.allenandunwin.com

National Library of Australia
Cataloguing-in-Publication entry:

Weiss, Rachael, 1964- .
    Are we there yet? : Rach and Jules take to the open road.

    ISBN 1 74114 377 2.

    1. Single women - Humor. 2. Women travelers - Australia.
    3. Voyages and travels - Humor. I. Adams, Julie. II.
    Title.

910.4082

Set in 10/15.12 pt La Gioconda by Bookhouse, Sydney
Printed in Australia by McPherson's Printing Group

10 9 8 7 6 5 4 3 2

*This book is dedicated to the glorious
Barbara Lasserre*

Contents

CHAPTER ONE

Yup, still single

⌐⊙ ❦ **Jules and Rach contemplate single life**

Are you single? We are, and we're not happy about it. We spend a lot of time thinking about it and talking about it. In the last week we've talked about almost nothing else. We've tried to look on the bright side. Being single's not so bad most of the time—we're free as the birds (not the caged ones, obviously), we have regular lives with no domestic dramas. We sleep and eat whenever we feel like it and we never have to worry about nappies, school lunches or the Great Toilet Seat Debate.

But there are many very annoying things about being a single girl. No sex, for a start. No-one to stay at home with on a Saturday night. No-one to complain to during the week when your boss is being irritating. And that tiring feeling of being unsupported: you have to do everything in your life for yourself—do all the grocery shopping, hang the pictures, fix the washers, weed the garden, wash the car, put out the garbage. We're marvellously empowered, of course, and running with the wolves along the road less travelled like mighty urban Amazons, but just once in a while it would be nice to say, 'Sorry, I don't know how to fix a washer—could you please do it, honey?' Or even less PC: 'The garbage is the man's domain—off you go.' Dear oh dear, whatever would Germaine Greer say? Well, whatever she'd say, who cares? It's true!

And life is full of embarrassing moments when you're a single woman, especially if you're desperate not to be. If you're not crying into your pillow in utter despair, you're making a complete klutz of yourself over those rare candidates who suddenly appear—who are the right age, have a brain and can play a decent game of Scrabble. Of the two of us, Jules tends to get out and about and meet people so she gets to have her hopes dashed frequently and her heart broken periodically. Rach avoids this by studiously ignoring social activities, devoting her leisure hours to films with girlfriends or staying home. That way she is magnificently unprepared for the shock of meeting a potential candidate. This lack of match practice means Rach manages to bring shame and ignominy to her family name by the lengths to which desperation will drive her on those rare, rare occasions she meets a man she actually likes. Why only the other day . . . but we'll let Rach tell you in her own words.

👓 Rach does a brave, yet foolish, thing

Last Monday, I gave a guy my phone number. Boy, am I glad I did that. Because now, exactly one week and 23 hours has passed and I haven't heard from him. One day and no call, okay; two days and no call, slightly less okay, but still doable; three days and I know this is going to be unpleasant. On day three, my gay friends said to me, 'One week and he's interested, two weeks and he's so-so, three weeks, forget it.' But I disagree. Two days is all he gets to be cool, after that he's either not interested or he's playing games. Either way, he's not going to be The One. Day four and I was really, really sad.

As the days went by, I imagined what I'd say when he phoned. The first two days it's 'Hiii' in a soft tone because, well, he's called, and possibility has begun. On day three, it's distracted, like 'Oh, hi'—a tiny bit surprised to hear from him. Day five, and I'm getting that heavy-hearted feeling, but I'm not admitting it to myself yet, so when he calls I'm laughing heartily with friends as I answer the phone—'Hello? Who? Oh, hi'—still with a laugh in my voice and happy to hear from him, because my life is full, like one day, five days it's all the same to me, because I'm cool about everything. Day seven and it's 'Who? Oh, right, how are you?' like after so much time, you don't really expect me to remember you, do you?

Today (day eight, but who's counting) I had lunch with two straight guys from my office. Straight guys aren't like gay guys—they understand straight men. I said, 'It's been a week!' They gave each other the Look. 'This is a girl world/guy world thing,' they said. 'That's nothing. A week is three hours in men's time. A week with no phone call? That doesn't mean anything.'

So I started to feel better. Maybe I'd been fretting over nothing. Of course! I forgot to account for the different time zones! I'm judging him by girl world time. What do gay guys know, anyway? It's really only been three hours. I'm happy again.

'Perhaps he's shy,' said my adorable, straight male friends. I said, 'Do you think? He's a detective—surely there's no such thing as a shy detective.' The guys gave each other the Look again. *What? What's the Look for?* 'Detective . . . that's bad. Coppers can have any woman they want,' said one of them. 'Yeah, women love coppers,' said the other. They shook their heads, 'You don't want to go near this one.' And I knew they were right, just like they were right about the time zones. And then I was really depressed.

Then one of these insensitive dolts launched into a story about a detective he lived with who had women coming around to his house all the time, just to get laid. 'I've seen him with three different women in one day. All married.' *Shut up, Ray.* 'It's incredible. I don't know what it is about coppers, but women are all over them.' He carried on happily with his ridiculous tale. Honestly. Men.

So I went back to my office and I cried. Because I'm 35 and, despite the fact that one week and 23 hours has passed, and there's been no call, I still carry my phone around with me and every time it rings, I hope. Just then, I thought I heard the phone, and I jumped, yes *jumped*, up to get it before I remembered that I'd turned it off.

It makes no sense, except that the thing about this guy was that I actually thought I might be able to talk to him for the rest of my life. And I haven't met a single guy I could talk to for the rest of my life since June 14, 1998. That's when I started going out with Byron, my last boyfriend. Pity he turned out to be a faithless, lying, womanising alcoholic. Don't look at me like that—it's true. Byron would be the first to agree with this description—he's a very fair man. He's funny, smart, incisive, and drunk most of the time. We had one glorious year where we never left each other's sight, and then about three years of utter misery trying to untangle ourselves from a ghastly mess. Even that was all right, because at least I had him there to talk to, well okay, occasionally scream at, but *there. Mine.*

Now I come to think about it, all my boyfriends have been lunatics in one way or another. What made me think a guy I could talk to for the rest of my life would be a lovely, stable, committed sort of chap? I must be mad for even contemplating a relationship with someone I like talking to. My radar has unfailingly spotted drunken mongrels and shows no sign of repairing itself.

♟ Jules offers the philosophical perspective

Rach is right. Her radar is crap. But mine isn't, and still I can't get a date. What is it with the modern world? How can there be so many of us, men and women, so very, very unhappily single? Is it a new disease? Have we forgotten the art of marriage? Maybe it has something to do with our incredible wealth. We can have everything—a house, warmth, food, safety, a satisfying career, hot and cold running entertainment at the flick of a switch—now all we need is love.

I thought I'd delay having children and put my youthful energy to really good use—like partying myself senseless all over the world. I thought I'd wait until I found my twin soul, the man who had everything—looks, a good job, money, sense of humour, thoughtful pleasant nature, world-class sexual technique, inability to think about more than one woman at a time (me), engaging conversationalist, sensitive, deep, artistic, intuitive, emotionally mature, in touch with his feminine side. Yes, that's the man for me. Imagine my surprise when, at around 31 or so, my dating options began to dry up. To my amazement, most men who fell into the 'possible' category were now married. Or, in Sydney, gay. Or, again in Sydney, both. Left in the 'available' category were the laughably unlikely—the poor sods who'd clearly been utterly ruined by appalling parents who'd taught them zero social skills. I'd pity them but then I remember that these are the ones who buy mail-order brides and get someone to love the easy way. Pity them? They're having sex. I have superb social skills and no sex. Who's laughing now?

'Are we lonely singles asking too much of the world?' I put this question to Rach. 'What with all this wealth and opportunity, the pressure on us to make the most of everything is huge. We've got jobs and friends and white goods, so if we're not having a good time—laughing, free, windswept and loved—something must be wrong with us. I feel like I've failed. I've got all this good stuff and still I yearn for a mate. We think that when we meet The One, all our problems will be solved. But can this be true? For a start, is every one of us going to meet that wonderful, fictional character, the Twin Soul? Some of us do, and we all hope like hell that *we* will be one of the lucky ones, but what if we don't? What happens then?'

Rach agreed with me. She thinks that The One is a fiction designed to keep us in a state of eternal dissatisfaction. It's a capitalist ploy to keep us buying shoes we don't need.

'Jules, think about it,' said Rach. 'How many people do you know whose marriages are held together by about three bottles of red wine a night and an utter blinder every weekend? I can name you half a dozen without even thinking. How many people actually meet Mr Right?'

'It seems so unfair, doesn't it,' I said. 'You can meet Mr Alcoholic easily enough. Mr All Consuming Ego populates most offices, and Mr Tedium won't stop calling. Mr Completely Out Of The Question But Convinced You Are His Twin Soul is one charge sheet short of an AVO if he doesn't stop coming around to my office. But Mr Right? In hiding, apparently. An undercover agent. Testing out a new formula for invisibility he's just invented.'

The point is, do you know anyone who's fully happy? Truly contented with their lot? Our friend George Taxi, well-known Sydney cabby identity, put this question to us. It took some thought but the answer is: No. No, we don't know anyone who is actually content. What sort of state of affairs is that? How can we be living in such unparalleled wealth and freedom and still be unhappy? Perhaps it all comes from inside—all this choice and responsibility that freedom brings with it has blighted our fragile psyches. Clearly, some people have the gift for true happiness—we don't know any of them but they write enough books on the subject, so there must be some.

Another glass of chardy, Rach? Don't mind if I do, Jules.

¥ Jules does strength training with George

I thought I'd pursue happiness through strength training with George Taxi. George believes in the power of exercise to keep you hanging in there. He is a single man, who has renounced love as the source of all agony and is devoting himself to the care of Kitty, his cat. Originally named Namronette Kitten Seven—Space Kitten with a Mission, for reasons which have disappeared into the mists of time (probably a dodgy acid tab), Kitty is the most petted cat you're ever likely to meet. She gets the finest sashimi known to mankind for every meal. She has a favourite spot on a window ledge in the living room where she likes to get warm in the morning. George has noticed that it doesn't get the sun for very long, so if Kitty's there at breakfast time, rather than make her waste valuable heating time by coming to her bowl, George will stand outside the window, hand feeding her fresh fish while she lies back sunning herself.

At the end of each shift, at four o'clock in the morning, George Taxi takes Kitty for a walk in the park, carefully shielding her from the attentions of other cats. Actually, Kitty is barking mad so other cats steer clear anyway, bearing in mind that old jail tag—it's not the strongest you have to worry about, it's the craziest. It's not safe for anyone except George to tickle Kitty behind the ears—she'll have your hand off in a second. Rach and I have friends in Cowra and we frequently ask George to come visiting with us, but he can't leave the house overnight. Why not? Because apparently no-one has the requisite skills to look after Kitty in the manner to which she is accustomed. We say, George, old man, she's a cat. You could give her a good feed, put her outside for the night, and she'd still be there the next day when you got home. George frostily asks us never to speak in that unfeeling manner again.

George became my exercise buddy. I picked George Taxi because he is a maniac, but a good and faithful maniac who will always be ready to lash me into a sweat if it looks like I'm taking it easy in the gym.

It does do you good to be a bit fit. It's hard to keep it up and there are days when I call George to say I've got to work back at the office when really I just have to veg on the couch with a packet of Tim Tams, but on the whole a healthy mind actually is given a head start by a healthy body. I only had one complaint, and that was the fact that George chose City Gym for our fitness regimen. City Gym! I ask you. If I'm going to get sweaty in a leotard could I at least go to a gym where *straight* guys can see me?

George has just called to tell me that he's adjusting our path slightly to incorporate the True Path—yogic self-realisation. Where we have been crudely adding lumps of muscle to our bodies, we are now going to gently stretch and strengthen, contacting the luminous child within when we perform the Down Dog. Forming a perfect triangle with our butts pointing to the ceiling, we will see into the eternal light. Even George couldn't keep a straight face.

But as you well know, exercise only gets you so far. Especially if you're hanging out at City Gym. Okay, I've put away the razor blades, but I'd still like a date now I'm all toned and buff. Or anyway, between now and when my next ice-cream bender undoes all the good work.

Thelma gives us a shove

Contemplating our loveless state, we realise that our social lives aren't even as full as Thelma's (she lives with Rach). Once, when we were watching *Terms of Endearment* for the twentieth time and sobbing into our Herb and Spice Kettle Chips, Thelma gatecrashed a party the boys upstairs in no. 3 were throwing. Just strolled in like she owned the joint, plonked herself on the couch in the middle of the action and demanded attention. Which she got. Everyone loved her and she was the centre of attention. She even made it into the boys' home videos. This was all weeks, mind you, *weeks* before we even knew there *were* two guys living in no. 3.

Thelma first came to live with Rach eleven and a half years ago, apparently on a mission from God to keep Rach and her surroundings covered in a fine layer of ginger fur. She's an affectionate little thing, though, so Rach keeps feeding her and providing her with scratching posts—which she ignores in favour of the couch, now more rag than sofa.

Thelma can't imagine a life where she's anything but solo. It's all right for a free spirit like her, roaming the nightspots, having it off with any guy she meets. She's a girl who can take it or leave it, and mostly she leaves it, which is apparently the come-on of a lifetime. Sometimes her boyfriends serenade her at night, but Rach finds a bucket of water generally gets the message across. Thelma gives her a look, but since we all know she's not interested we fail to see the problem.

When Rach told her she needed a holiday, of course Thelma could only whine about who would look after her. She's the most selfish creature we've ever met. We tell her that the entire world is not here to indulge her every whim, so she turns her back on us and walks off in a huff. Sarah Bernhardt lives.

Rach is right. We need a break. It's time to find the child within, or at least a couple of cases of '98 Hunter Valley reds. If we can't have love we're going to have a holiday, but not one where we come back even more miserable at our loveless lives. Holidays can be treacherous like that. Jules read the other day that in the modern world people are working longer hours and avoiding holidays. The 'people' in question would be all us singlettes who would rather not be reminded that work is the most fulfilling relationship we have. Let's face it, if we were a happy couple, we'd plan a trip to the Great Barrier Reef together, looking forward to spending time in each other's company away from the pressures of work, renewing our relationship. One of us would find accommodation, the other would book the tickets, then we'd fly off together to indulge in a week of sun, snorkelling and sex. On our return, we'd tell all our friends about it. 'We' did this and 'we' did that; how single girls do tire of that 'we'.

No, what *we* need for this holiday is a single chick haven. We need a place to go where we won't be surrounded by smug couples on a second honeymoon. So we've decided we'll go on a road trip. We'll head south through the Highlands, make a loop through our National Capital, head north through the Blue Mountains and maybe visit our Three Spinster Sisters, then on to the vineyards of the Hunter Valley and end with a luxury stop at Terrigal. Our mission— to find the secret of happiness, to discover the true meaning of life, to bring joy and fulfilment to our single lives. Or, failing that, to come back with a halfway decent tan and a truckload of booze for Jules' cellar.

CHAPTER TWO

We run away from home

⊖ 🍸 Thelma and Louise

There's nothing more exciting than setting off on a road trip. For two glorious weeks we're going to forget about work, leave all care behind, run away from the empty routine of our lives and pretend we are Thelma and Louise, minus the assault and descent into a criminal vortex, of course. Come to think of it, what did that film tell us single chicks? It told us marriage is a depressing if not downright violent state of affairs, to be avoided at all costs; it said that should you ever try to free yourself from the chains of your life you will be hunted down and forced to choose between suicide and jail; if you meet a man and he's cute he'll steal your wallet, if he's a good dancer he'll rape you; if two women hold hands just before driving off a cliff to their certain deaths, film critics will spend years wondering if they were really gay; and setting fire to trucks is fun. And yet, whenever women set off on a road trip we put on headscarves and dark glasses and say, 'We're like Thelma and Louise'. For all the unpleasantness with the law, nothing can erase the feeling of utter freedom in the film, and secretly don't we all rather wish we could be on a road trip forever?

The first day is the best, because you have the whole trip of limitless possibilities before you. Bit like life, really. The Sydney philosopher David Stove once told Rach that it is the natural course of mankind (his word, he was an old-fashioned guy) to begin life believing fervently in free will—we all have the power to be and do whatever we want. And then as life closes in, mankind becomes less sure about this free will thing and is more inclined to think that it is all preordained and that one couldn't possibly have wished this on oneself. By the end, one believes that a force greater than oneself, with a pretty questionable sense of humour, has organised the lot from the beginning. This may explain the mid-life crisis. We get to about 40 and think, Oh crap, halfway through and not famous, rich, beautiful, happy, fulfilled or wise. Bugger. Did I do this? No! *God* did it. Wait—I don't believe in God. Bugger.

🍸 Jules picks up Rach at the crack of a sparrow's

We always take my car because mine is the biggest and has a CD player. Both of us like to get out on the highway in the early morning light, so on the first day of our trip I was at Rach's place at six am, just as she emerged from her flat decked out in a miniskirt and oversized handbag.

'Hilloooo!' I gave her the cheery welcome.

'Hilloooo!' she cried. 'Ready to leave all care and worry behind?'

'Sure am. Where's your luggage, hon?'

'Here,' Rach indicated the handbag she was carrying. She seemed surprised by my question.

'What? That's it? Rach, where's your overcoat?'

'It's September,' she said. 'Why would I need an overcoat?'

'It's thirteen degrees in Canberra. Did you bring long pants?'

'No.'

'So what's in the bag?'

'Another skirt and a few tops. And underwear.'

'And is your other skirt a mini as well?'

Pause.

'Possibly.'

'Rach, go back inside and get proper clothes. You'll need an overcoat, long pants, a jumper, maybe a spencer, socks, a long skirt, stockings, something to wear when we go out in the evenings, evening shoes, sandals, walking shoes . . .'

'And I've just remembered that I've forgotten the camping gear.' Was she even listening to me?

I sighed, 'Oh, yes. The camping gear.' I'm not much of a fan of camping. Rach loves it, though.

'Jules, don't tell me *you've* brought all that stuff,' said Rach.

'Of course I have. And swimmers, a beach towel, sarong, beach wear, the beach umbrella, eskies for picnics at the beach . . .'

'Are we going to the beach?'

'We're going to Terrigal—there's a beach there. We may want the beach experience, and if we do we're going to need the equipment. Gym gear, gym shoes, riding helmet, jodhpurs, riding boots, thick walking socks, a bushwalking shirt, suncream, after-sun lotion . . .'—but I'd lost my audience. Rach had disappeared inside.

She came out five minutes later with her tent and camping gear. I opened my mouth to tell her she'd need a bit more than that, but she waved me quiet—she'd got the point. Fifteen minutes later, and one large-ish bag heavier, Rach and I were ready to hit the road.

⌐ ∵ We have no shame at all about Our Anthem

'Really, Rach,' said Jules, 'what were you thinking? Two miniskirts for Canberra? You'd have caught your death.'

'I guess. It just seemed so hot this morning.'

'You packed this morning?' Jules was appalled.

'Sure,' said Rach. 'When did you pack?'

'I was all done three days ago. What are you laughing about?'

'Nothing. Ooh, the freeway. Time for freeway music, I think. What'll we have?'

We both knew the answer to that question, but we like to pretend that we're not totally predictable.

'*The Big Chill*?'

'Nah. Kylie?'

'Mmmm . . . no.'

'Then I think we only have one option . . .' Rach slid a disc into the CD player, and as the music started we joined in at the tops of our voices. Due to seatbelt restraints we couldn't do the dance moves that every ABBA-lovin' girl perfects at nine years old, but we could, and did, faithfully reproduce the authentic finger movements as we bawled, '*You* can dance! *You* can ji-ive! *Having* the time of your li-i-ife! Ooh ooh ooh! *See* that girl! *Watch* that scene, diggin' *the dancing queen!*'

We sailed down the M5, the wind in our hair, the sun on our faces, and a song on our lips. Ah, road music. Luckily we are as one on the subject of road music—it must be loud and it must be ABBA. Or Kylie, Robbie Williams, Frank, *The Big Chill* soundtrack and, lately, Norah Jones. Knowledge of the words is not as important as enthusiasm, flair and volume.

The role of the passenger

On every road trip it is the passenger's responsibility to take care of the driver. The passenger must pass opened bottles of drink at regular intervals, unwrap chocolate bars and provide essential energy supplements to the driver to keep up their strength. Jelly Snakes are the best, but make sure you get the good ones. It is also the passenger's duty to navigate.

'Where's the map?' asked Rach.

'Glovebox,' replied Jules. 'I've done one for each leg of the trip.'

Rach looked surprised, 'We're not using the old one?'

'I found these on the web.'

'Cool,' said Rach, removing a sheaf of papers from the glovebox.

'They're in order,' said Jules, keeping her eyes on the road. 'Sydney to Berrima's on top.'

Rach studied the top map. Then she studied Jules.

'It's time for the men in white coats, Jules.'

'What do you mean?' Jules sounded surprised.

'This isn't a road map of Sydney to Berrima, these are instructions from my door to the door of Berkelouw's Book-shop. With times for each leg. Jules, it says here, "Turn left out of driveway on to Mountain St travelling south to Warrawong Rd. 20 sec." *20 sec?* "Turn left into Warrawong Rd, travel east to Marrickville Rd. 3 min 30 sec." Have you gone completely mad?'

'What's wrong with times? This way we can gauge how much time we have to stop at places.' Jules valiantly defended the indefensible.

'What are you like at work, Jules? No, I really want to know.'

'Hey! If you want to take care of the maps, you can. But you don't—I do. So I've taken advantage of modern technology to upgrade us from our scuzzy old map of New South Wales, covered in yellow highlighter and mostly obliterated by the giant coffee stain splashed across it from the time you tried to drive, drink a cappuccino and turn the map the right way around all at the same time!'

And with that she closed her case, for on the subject of navigation the whole world agrees that Jules has the upper hand. She's been a tour guide and so can actually read a map. Rach on the other hand can barely distinguish a map from, say, a sci-fi novel, although she secretly thinks the whole world underestimates her directional ability.

The Holiday Buddy System and how we got here

We are Holiday Buddies. Like a lot of singlettes we both figure out what we are missing by not being in a relationship, then we try to manufacture it. We find someone to go to the gym with, someone to complain to about work, someone to holiday with, someone to buy a house with. The synthetic variety never seems as good as the natural, home-grown variety we think we long for, but it sure beats nothing at all.

We met ten years ago when Rach was temping in the public service and Jules was a permanent public servant about to be 'restructured'. (The actual department had better remain nameless unless we want the proceeds of this book to go to our legal fees.) We got to talking and found that we were both single, both desperate for a date and both living in Sydney's inner west. Neither of us had been on a holiday in over a year, because we didn't have anyone to go with. We went on complaining to each other for some time before it occurred to us that all we had to do was go together and our problem was solved. We decided that as soon as Jules' employer had finished caringly assisting her in her outplacement journey, we'd go on a holiday. We did, and that was the start of our long and happy Holiday Buddy relationship. Actually, the story of the end of Jules' job security is quite amusing . . .

☒ Jules gets restructured

It's a funny thing working in a unit that's losing money. In the public service that doesn't necessarily mean the end of the unit—if it did, that would be the end of the public service. (Just kidding officer, the APS is a fine institution.) Anyhow, I was working in the business development unit of a government department that was running out of money faster than most. This wasn't a problem for the first two Directors, who were both career bureaucrats, but the third Director wasn't used to the culture. Instead of explaining to the Under Secretary why the unit was actually *making* money by trading at a loss, he got flustered and blamed the staff. That gave the Under Secretary the excuse he needed and the decision was made to wind us up.

We were all called into his office and told that our unit was being dissolved, that we would be re-deployed *where possible* (ominous phrase) and that until the department had decided what to do with us we must maintain absolute secrecy. Don't want to upset the troops, that sort of thing. We glumly agreed and plodded back to our office to polish up our CVs. As we opened the office door, I nearly tripped over Fred from Facilities who was on his knees fiddling with a measuring tape.

'What are you doing, Fred?' I asked. 'Are we getting new furniture?'

'Ha ha ha, that's a good one. Glad to see you've kept your sense of humour. No, I'm measuring up for new partitions the Accounting Unit's ordered,' he said, jovially.

'And when will Accounting be moving into this space?' I asked, with an air of guileless innocence I have developed over many years in the service.

'Oh, plans are for the end of the month, but I should think that's hopeful,' said Fred. 'Sorry to hear you ladies are leaving us. Got a job to go to, have you?'

As a friend of mine in the Finance Unit said, if the Minister tells you, take it with a grain of salt, but if the cleaners tell you, you know it's true.

The end of the month did turn out to be a bit of a pipedream for the poor old Accounting Unit. You've heard the battle cry of the public service, haven't you—'What do we want?' *'Gradual change!'* 'When do we want it?' *'In due course!!'*—nothing ever happens fast in the public service. So for nine months, we languished in limbo land while the public service passed endless bits of paper to itself trying to work out how to finish off a business unit. And while they were doing that, the unit died a natural death, so no-one had to do anything after all. Still, I'll say this for the public service—it builds patience and endurance. Not to mention an astounding ability to drink many, many chardies on a Friday night.

And I'd keep on telling you this story but Rach seems to have buried herself in the map trying to figure out whether we go left or right at Mittagong. She's got it on the car seat and is trying to turn herself in the direction we're going. I point out the giant green sign that tells us where to turn off. *Mittagong, Bowral, Moss Vale and Berrima—Welcome to the Southern Highlands.* Rach looks relieved and happy.

'I got us there!' I let her enjoy the triumph of having success-
fully navigated us straight down the Hume Highway.

Berrima, Berkelouw's Bookshop and the Tidy Town phenomenon

Mind you, this is not the first time we have come to Berrima.
In fact, it's the twelfth. Yes, the twelfth, and still Rach doesn't
know the turn off! Whatever. We aren't so much visiting Berrima
as paying homage to Berkelouw's Bookshop, which is on the
old Hume Highway just before you get to Berrima. Or rather,
I'm letting Rach pay homage as she is obsessed with books.
I keep meaning to check the *Diagnostic Manual IV* to see
if there is a disease where people confuse reading with living
because I'm sure all this reading and book collecting can't
be quite normal. We've been on about fifteen holidays
together and nearly every one has had to start with a loop
via Berrima so Rach can hunt for first editions the proprietors
of Berkelouw's have accidentally underpriced.

The great thing about this bookshop is that it's a huge
country house surrounded by farmland. I remembered this
just in time this morning, and I've brought my golf clubs
with me. I've had quite enough of Berkelouw's but my
backswing has gone haywire recently so, while Rach is on
her knees closely inspecting jacket covers, I'll be in an
adjoining pasture aiming for the nearest gum tree. And I've
got a treat for her, although . . . well, I'll tell you later. First,
to give Rach the good news.

'I thought we might stay in Berrima tonight,' I said, 'so
you can have more time browsing.'

Her face lit up like a lift that's stopping at every floor.

'Do you mean that? Really?'

'Really. I'm always hustling you out of there just when you're getting into the zone. So, I'll go into town and book a motel, shall I? Meet you back here in, say, four hours?'

'I might just have covered the fiction section by then. But if not, there's always tomorrow morning!' And with that she bounded up the steps three at a time and dived through the front door.

I drove into Berrima to find a motel and the coffee I sorely needed after two and a half hours on the road. It's a sweet old place Berrima, and—typical of Australian country towns that make their living off the tourist trade—it's stuffed full of old courthouses, post offices, and banks covered in plaques which tell you exactly who was hanged on this spot, or what was invented. The trouble with Australia is that it's just not old enough to have any historical interest whatsoever, so if you're a tourist town you really have to squeeze every last drop of historical romance out of your buildings that you can. Berrima lays claim to the oldest jail in country New South Wales, the oldest pub in the Southern Highlands and the last spot Burke and Wills were seen before disappearing into the desert (or was that Charles Wentworth? Oh well, there's a plaque somewhere in town that'll tell you all about it). Every second store in town sells homemade jam and chutneys, and the ubiquitous Devonshire tea.

I'll say this for it, though—I've yet to see a sign claiming Berrima is a Tidy Town winner (1991), which is amazing, since every other country town in Australia seems to claim it won Tidy Town of 1991. Rach and I have spotted so many we believe the Tidy Town committee of 1991 was as corrupt as 1920s Chicago. Did the bloke next door to you get a sudden windfall in 1991? Put up a gazebo when only the month before he'd lost his job? Check the records, my friend—odds are he was a Tidy Town judge . . . You heard it here first.

Luckily, our little country towns do coffee to die for. I think it's one of Australia's crowning achievements that you have to travel right into the Red Centre before the coffee gets instant and undrinkable. I've travelled the world, and I can tell you that in London, where they have history coming out their turrets, you can't get a decent coffee even in the best international hotels. The café owners of Berrima like to give you a Devonshire tea with your coffee, of course. There's so much Devonshire tea around you'd think it was the staple diet of the locals. There's not a café that doesn't advertise the stuff. But I'm fond of the odd scone with jam and cream, so I sat myself down for a reviving cappuccino and accessories.

After my coffee I found us not a motel, but a cheap B&B, booked us in, then went back to Berkelouw's for some golf practice. I gave Rach plenty of time to ferret around in the bookshop, in fact until nigh on dusk, which was pretty gener-ous of me but, as I mentioned before, I had an ulterior motive. When I finally went in to scoop her out from behind Maps and Atlases she had the dazed look of a chocaholic who'd got lost in the Cadbury's factory and hadn't been found for a fortnight. I steered her out of the shop and into the car while she babbled on about her collection of Georgette Heyer first editions and showed me a hardback featuring a smouldering hero and fainting heroine she'd picked up for $4.95.

'Do you realise what this costs on eBay? In this mint condition? $25 US at least, and look at this!' She waved a clearly very ancient and somewhat water-damaged book at me, 'It's the *Storia Ecclesiastica*, printed in 1778!'

'It's in Italian,' I said. 'I didn't know you could read Italian.'

'I can't. But I can read Roman numerals—this book was printed in 1778, Jules, *1778*! And look what else I found— Quiller-Couch's *Oxford Book of English Verse*. Okay, it's a 1949 edition, but look at the condition! It's perfect!'

And so it went on. She's nothing if not catholic in her literary tastes. I let her take me through her purchases one by one then, at the first pause, I moved the subject along to our slight change of plans. Now, I felt, was a good time to broach the little problem.

'I've booked us into a B&B. It's terribly doily-covered and I fear it will be infested with lovesick couples, but we're only there for a night, and it was cheap,' I said that last bit advisedly.

'Oh well, just for one night it can't hurt,' she said. 'We'll have each other if it turns out to be a hornet's nest of couples, and cheap is good.'

'Yes, it is, isn't it? Cheap is good. Cheap is very good. We'll have one or two expensive stops, so we'll save where we can, even if it means fluffy toys on the bed.'

'One or two? What do you mean "one or two"? I thought our only extravagance was going to be Terrigal?'

'It is. It is. It's just that we might find that we have unexpectedly booked into a place that is perhaps a little more exxy than we'd planned on.'

'What?'

I took a breath. Now was the time to give her the bad news about our next stop. 'The health retreat isn't $120 for two nights. It's $210.'

'What?'

'Each.'

'What??!!'

'Per night.'

'WHAT!!!'

'I know you hate to spend money, but really, Rach, it'll be worth it! They have spas and massages and facials and a swimming pool.'

'$210 PER NIGHT?? Does George Clooney come with that? Because that's the only thing that'll justify those prices! That's highway robbery.'

'It's not, you know. Plenty of places cost that and more. That's the price of luxury, Rach.'

'I hate luxury! Luxury leaves me cold! Bugger luxury! People think if they call it luxury they can charge prices you'd expect on the Space Shuttle. Luxury is an outrageous and overrated con.'

'Yes, but I need it, I really do,' I played my trump card. 'I'm desperate for pampering. Work has been terrible in the last few weeks. I haven't slept properly for ages.' I knew she'd be too kind-hearted to make a fuss if I pleaded stress and overwork.

There was a short, seething silence while Rach tried to harden her resolve. Then she sighed. 'Right-o then, $210 per night per person it is. But if it's not top notch stuff I reserve the right to complain loudly.'

'Done!' And I was very relieved, because she really does hate to spend money and there was a chance she could have simply refused to go.

After a moment, Rach said, 'So that explains my extended trip to Berkelouw's. Softening me up were you?'

Oops. Should've known she'd put two and two together. 'Nothing of the sort! I just thought you'd like . . . oh, all right then, yes.' She was giving me a quizzical look and I couldn't keep up the pretence. 'But I promise you, you'll like it.'

'Yeah, yeah. At least I'll have some good reading material.'

And with that we were back to normal.

The Berrima B&B and the pitfall we should have seen

Jules had indeed found us a frightfully squishy little place in the heart of Berrima (a place that I am quite sure thought of itself without shame as THE heart of Berrima). It was one of those B&Bs that pays homage to the frilly-curtains-and-knickknacks style of interior decoration. The place was stuffed full of pastel soft furnishings and paintings of kittens cuddling up to Alsatians. Every conceivable surface was covered in gathered muslin. On top of the muslin, small jars of potpourri fought for space with china figurines, velvet heart-shaped boxes, artfully placed ribbons, dolls in white nineteenth century dresses, and local homemade jams with labels hand-written in copperplate. The owner was a soft, squishy woman in her mid-fifties with big, soft, entreating blue eyes and a floating white skirt. I loathed her on sight.

I keep saying 'soft' and 'squishy'—I can't help it, I just can't get those two words out of my mind in connection with this awful place. I mentioned this to Jules who refrained from telling me to quit moaning, which she usually does, only because, speaking of 'soft', she was still trying to soften me up after her health retreat debacle. Honestly, $210 per night—each! It's an outrage.

Anyhow, as we were staggering up the porch steps under a hundredweight of Jules' luggage, which she claimed we'd need 'just in case', I heard a noise on the verandah. I dropped my end of the load and brushed the wisteria out of my eyes to see that the noise was the creak of a porch swing, and on the swing was a young couple, holding hands and gazing. Not gazing at the moon, which was there for them to gaze at, but at us, and seemingly in some annoyance at our turning their scented evening tryst into a removalists' convention. Jules stopped when I stopped and looked at the couple too. They gazed back, their annoyance palpable. Jules sent her end of the bag crashing to the ground after mine and said, chirpily, 'Hello! Lovely spot you've got here!'

And the Male Half mumbled, 'Yes, wasn't it?' while the Female Half simply looked put out.

'Staying here long?' She can be quite naughty when she's annoyed, our Jules.

'Not long, no,' said the Male Half, forced into politeness. Female Half turned her gaze to the rose bushes in the twilight.

'Picked a lovely night for a swing on the porch!' Was she to have no mercy on them? I was enjoying this hugely.

'Mmmm,' said Female Half, nestling into Male Half.

Jules hauled at her luggage with extra enthusiasm, putting a lot of grunt into heaving it back up off the porch. Female Half sighed loudly and Male Half picked up her hand.

'See you at dinner, then!' cried Jules with hearty menace, and we lumbered inside under our burden.

'Really, Jules! And you have the gall to call *me* rude.'

'Well, I don't like it when couples claim territory. It's a porch, for chrissakes! So we were on it at the same time, spoiling their atmosphere. Too bad. They didn't need to give us a Look. I object to Looks. Don't like something, then say so, but do not Look.'

As she was saying this, she was trying to get the key in the lock to open the door to our room. Since it was an old-fashioned iron key you'd normally associate with castle gates, this was no easy task. They'd whipped out all the Mr Minit locks and replaced them with Mr 1574 locks in the interest of atmosphere. Poor Jules was getting quite agitated, which isn't at all like her.

'Flippin' 'eck!' she said. (Isn't that sweet? She hasn't said the F-word since her first niece was born.) 'What is the story with this lock? Turn, yer mongrel!'

At that moment, the Courting Couple from the porch came in from the twilight and, hearing this and seeing Jules wrestling madly with the lock, gave each other a long-suffering look—the heathens had invaded Paradise. I smiled at them, really to make up for Jules, and they gave me a slight grimace. Right, that's the last niceness they get out of me.

'At last!' The lock gave and we fell into our room. We

hauled the case in and collapsed onto our beds, another reason I can't get the words 'soft' and 'squishy' out of my mind.

'Jules,' I said, my voice slightly muffled by the mattress which had risen like displaced water around me, 'why did you pick this place?'

'Cheap.'

'I wonder if I'm inclined to place too much emphasis on price? Don't think me critical, but next time we see lace curtains and a porch swing, could we not?'

'Fine by me.' She was squirming on her bed with her hand underneath her back trying to get purchase on the clouds of eiderdown. 'There's something digging into my spine,' and she pulled out a teddy bear.

'Oh, sweeeet,' I cried. 'There's a whole row of them on the dresser—did you see?'

'God, this is awful.' But she started to laugh and then we were both in hysterics. We agreed that we had to get away from Honeymoon Central immediately. Just imagine actually dining here—we'd be carted home in straitjackets one day into our 'holiday to get away from it all'. If the atmosphere could rile even Jules, we were in mortal danger.

'Steak, I think, don't you, Rach?'

'Rare and bloody. Beer, pub, pool, possibly even pokies. Pity Berrima doesn't have an RSL. What we need is cheap, gawdy, bright lights and trashy, anything to wash off this sticky sweetness.'

So we dragged ourselves hand over hand out of the depths of the beds, navigated around Jules' trunk, fiddled the iron key in the door and made our way out to the car. As we passed through the wisteria I caught a glimpse of a courting couple on the porch swing. Not the same couple, a different couple. Two lots of hand-holding couples in the one B&B, and who knew how many more hidden inside. Oh yeah, we needed a steak, all right.

It wasn't easy finding gaudy and bright in Berrima. In fact, we didn't. We found any number of Historic Sandstone Inns, each with a different claim to fame—First to Open, Built by Convicts, Cobb & Co, Last to Close, Queen Victoria Blew Nose Here—and we settled in the end for one which seemed frequented by the more down-at-heel locals: people who are either married and escaping the family home for the night, or not married and keen to chat up a couple of strangers. The food was simple, cheap and good as it almost invariably is in country pubs, and we managed to ignore the coach lamps and cheer ourselves up with a couple of beers and a game of pool or two.

When we returned to the B&B, the moon was up, the air was heavy with scented flowers and a balmy breeze was blowing just enough to gently ruffle the hair. We surprised yet another couple on the porch swing, only this time they looked red-faced and confused rather than offended, since his hand was inside her shirt and her hand was inside . . . Dear Lord! We looked away quickly and crowded each other into the house.

'Remind me not to sit on that swing—I haven't had my shots.'

Jules wrestled with the key and took even longer this time, her brush with sex having utterly unnerved her. Jules is suffering a two-year drought and is acutely sensitive to sex in the air that is not being directed at her. We decided we needed to go to sleep immediately—the sooner to leave a place that was doing us no good at all—so we got into our pyjamas and climbed into bed. The mattresses folded around us like foot-thick hammocks and we lay snug in the dark exchanging snide comments about lace curtains and giggling.

Jules paused in the middle of a sentence. 'Rach, do you hear that?'

'I can barely hear *you* through this mattress. What is it?'

'That. Listen.'

I listened. *Creak, creak, creak.* 'What is it?'

'I *believe* it's the porch swing, and those creaks have a particular quality.'

Creakcreak. Creakcreak. Creakcreak.

'Oh dear. Outdoor sex.'

Creakcreakcreakcreakcreakcreakcreakcreak. There was a muffled groan.

'Oops, I bet that was sooner than he expected.' *Creakcreakcreakcreak.* Pause. *Creakcreakcreakcreak.*

'Well he's never going to make her come with a rhythm like that,' said Jules, 'You can't break it up. You've got to keep a steady pace.'

Creakcreakcreakcreak. Pause. *Creakcreakcreakcreak.*

'Shall I go out and mention it to him?'

'Too late now.'

Creakcreakcreakcreak. Pause. *Creakcreakcreakcreak.*

'He's not giving up though, is he?'

'You have to admire his stick-to-it-iveness.'

'So to speak.'

Creakcreakcreakcreak. Pause. *Creakcreakcreakcreak.*

'Oh, for God's sake, come already!'

'His thoughts as well, I'm sure. Although love is too new for him to admit it yet.'

'Cynic.'

There was a long silence, then the somewhat furtive sound of the front door opening.

'They've given up, then.'

'Or she's decided to at least get comfortable.'

Squeakchunk squeakchunk squeakchunk. The sound of a faux-distressed pine headboard on a shaky base beating regularly against a wall came to us from the room on our left.

'Gee, that was quick.'

'Christ, couldn't she just fake it so we can get some sleep?'

'Jules,' I said, in a voice of emerging horror, 'it's not them. I can hear the Porch Dwellers trying to break their room lock upstairs. It's *a different couple.*'

'Oh, for chrissakes, when is this going to be over? These two have just started and the other two haven't finished yet.'

Squeakchunk squeakchunk squeakchunk. Oh Oh Oh yeeeeeeees. Oh God Oh God. Oh just like that. Oh Oh Oh don't stop . . .

'No fear of that.'

'Great, a screamer.'

'Jules, *you're* a screamer.'

'I'm a considerate screamer. I scream in silence when other people are about. I mean, aren't these people embarrassed?'

Squeakchunksqueakchunksqueakchunk squeakchunk squeakchunk squeakchunk. Oh John. Oh God. Oh Oh Oh YEEEEEEEES.

'Apparently not.'

'I think I'll sing out "Hello John, get a good sleep last night, did you?" at breakfast tomorrow. Revenge.'

'Oh, do. It would make me so happy. You're so good at scenes.' And I meant it. Jules has no fear of confrontation whatsoever.

There was a longish silence.

'Sounds like it's all quiet for the night,' I said.

'Thank heavens for that.'

The night settled down around us and we began to drift off.

Squeakchunk squeakchunk squeakchunk.

'OH FOR GOD'S SAKE SHUT UP!'

And they did. Such is the power of a Jules enraged.

CHAPTER THREE

Luxury fails us

 We leave the soft and squishy B&B in a huff

The less said about the rest of that night the better. The Squeakchunkers weren't to be cowed for long and John's name was advertised to the whole world as a helluva man more than once. The Porch Dwellers got their rhythm going and kept it going. Their bed being as ricketty as the porch swing, we could spot the development of the young man's technique— no more *creakcreakcreak* pause *creakcreakcreak* pause. No, now he kept up a nice steady *creakcreakcreakcreakcreakcreak* all the goddamned night. At one point we heard a cooing sound and Jules bet it was the first couple we'd seen, adding to the chorus around us. We were both seething until I popped my head over the rim of the mattress and saw the source—a dove on our window sill. Words failed me.

What, it's not enough we should be tortured by the sounds of love and unstoppable passion all around us—now some universal fucking romantic icon is going to turn up looking smug and rubbing it in? This is bullshit, man! That fucking dove is lucky the only thing it got is a soft toy to the head. If I could have scrambled to the surface of the mattress quicker, it'd have been a dead dove. And don't ask me what I would have done with the head—just think *The Godfather* and beds.

We left the next morning as soon as the sun was up, making sure we sent Jules' trunk crashing to the ground more than once. Oops! Sorry, this trunk is sooooooo heavy— a little passive aggression to start the day. Our purpose was not really to be as annoying as possible—that was just a nice side effect—no, we just wanted to get out onto the open road, in the early morning sunshine, 'Dancing Queen' blasting from the speakers and the wind in our faces to try to wipe out the depressing effects of the night before.

As the country air took its effect, I said to Jules, 'We really must remember to avoid places which remind us we are single and loveless.'

'Yes, and that no-one wants to rip our clothes off and give us the night of our lives.'

'That too. Although, someone might want to do that, you just don't know about it.'

'They don't,' said Jules. 'I'd know. Thank God the retreat is next. You're going to love it. It'll be worth every cent, I promise. It'll be packed full of single women and we can lie back and be pampered in *complete* silence.'

'Ah, silence. A highly underrated attribute. Still—$210 per person per night.'

'You'll love it once you stop thinking about the money. Which you're going to do about now.'

Ah, silence. Apparently Jules required it so I obliged.

▼ The health retreat

The retreat is in the Southern Highlands, set in large grounds just outside Moss Vale. Its target market is the stressed out and overweight, and (according to Rach) the loaded and spoiled, although in her natural love of saving money, she exaggerates—there are plenty more expensive places. This retreat is on the lower end of the spectrum but it does have all the things you need if you're going to get de-stressed: a pool, a spa, a beauty therapist, a dietician, mudbaths, masseurs. I was as thrilled as a puppy that's just heard the work 'walkies'. Hoping Rach might catch the mood, I pointed out these benefits to her as we lugged our cases up the front steps.

'No porter, I notice,' sniffed Rach.

'Look at the view, isn't that gorgeous?'

'Hmmph. The verandah could do with a paint. Look, it's peeling.'

'Ooh. Floor-length velvet curtains! I love it.'

'Carpet's a bit threadbare.'

'Would you shut up and enjoy it, please?'

'Just making conversation.'

We were greeted at the front desk by a thin, impeccably

groomed woman in her well-preserved fifties. She looked like she'd just stepped out of an ad for Dove Moisturising Bar—all soft focus and apricot. She recognised straight away that I was the enthusiastic wife and Rach the long-suffering husband, and so confined her welcoming and brochure-thrusting to me while leading us up to our room. There, she showed us our bathroom (big enough to slightly mollify Rach) and the amenities—television, phone, minibar and more brochures showing us all the different ways the retreat could soothe away our cares. As soon as she left, I got on the phone and booked a full body massage, facial and manicure. Rach looked at the brochures, appalled.

'I don't believe it! They're charging for the treatments! On top of the $210.'

'Well, of course they are. What did you expect?'

'I *expected* George Clooney—I already told you that.'

'Why don't you do the free stuff? You've got the pool and the sauna and the hydro-bath, whatever that is. You can sit in the spa for as long as you like, then go out onto the verandah and read. No-one will make you talk to them—we're all here for the peace.'

'Hmmmm.'

She didn't sound convinced, but just then something caught her eye, 'Ooh. Jules, look. Is that a fluffy white bathrobe I spy on the door?'

'Why yes, ma'am. I believe it is.'

'How decadent. I rather fancy the idea of spending two days in swimmers and a fluffy white bathrobe. I can pretend I'm at the Betty Ford Clinic drying out, while nipping surreptitious swigs from the minibar.'

'Right, well, whatever toots your horn. I'm off to my full body experience with the resident Swedish masseur. Hope he's cute.'

'I'll cross my fingers for you. Why don't you go in the bathrobe? Get into the mood of the place.'

'And I do look rather fetching in white. Okay, deal. I'll meet you in the lounge this afternoon.'

'In your bathrobe?'

'In my bathrobe.'

Later that day . . .

We met, as arranged, in the lounge. Both of us had had our quiet time, I in the hands of the experienced, if regrettably female, Swedish masseuse and the nail artist, Rach in the spa and hammock communing with Georgette Heyer. Rach was right back in the holiday mood; she'd arrived at the lounge and found a cosy, quiet room with a fireplace, standard lamps and big comfy chairs—Rach heaven. She'd curled up on the leather couch in front of the fireplace and taken up her romance novel where she'd left off. When I joined her she was already up to the bit where the heroine discovers she does not really hate her guardian, the infuriatingly high-handed Lord Derringer, but is actually in love with him and has come insensibly to rely on his broad shoulders for support in coping with the shameful exploits of her drunken brother and fending off the unwelcome attentions of Baron Blastbutter. This, for those of you familiar with the romance genre, is a fair way into the book, so she was ready to return to the world of the living and indulge me in a fireside chat.

I, of course, was all for getting around a glass of white and into the evening's socialising, but I know Rach likes one-on-one time, so we chatted in quiet undertones on the couch. Just as I was starting to feel restless with all this inactivity, the cloistered late afternoon hush of the lounge was shattered by a cheery, smoker's voice hailing us from the door, 'Hello! New bugs!' Susie, a thin, taut-faced, excessively tanned woman looking awfully like Melanie Griffith during the surgery disasters, came sailing into the room, dressed not in the regulation fluffy whites, but a rather revealing, lacy and clearly very expensive negligee. Susie didn't seem to notice the still atmosphere in the room. She crashed onto the lounge next to me and began to regale us with a description of the other guests' maladies and intimate details of their private lives. I took this to be the start of the party and slipped into my well-practised social mode, listening to Susie and nodding and laughing in all the right places. However, I soon found that Susie didn't recognise the rules of social engagement. When I tried to reciprocate with a hilarious story of my own, Susie simply raised her voice. I was slightly startled, but I always like to give others the benefit of the doubt, so I simply continued the role of enthralled listener and ignored the tiny voice in my head that said, 'Life's too short.' Rach, on the other hand, was looking at Susie with undisguised horror.

'There's Lucy, who's here for her weight, poor dear, so she's on a juice only diet. Can you *imagine* that? She told me she'd been on the Soup Diet for *eight weeks* before she got here. Still the size of a luxury cruiser, though. Then there's Alice and Jean. Alice is recovering from the sudden death of her husband but since she'll be living off his assets—and he was worth *fifteen million*—for the rest of her life, without having to fuck anyone let alone a husband, I can't think what she could be recovering from. Jean is her best friend—a ghastly woman. And talk? Jean *never* shuts up. She *hogs* the conversation and bores on and on about some health problem she has which is why she's on the steamed vegetable cleansing diet.'

If what Susie said was true, then two things were clear: everyone else staying at the resort, including Susie, was apparently a raving lunatic and they were all on some ghastly diet or other. While I remained optimistic, I could see that Rach was beginning to wilt and feel distinctly depressed. Susie bashed on and on. We got to hear about the lawyer who'd had a nervous breakdown, the housewife who was here as a last resort before she died of boredom, the retreat's physical fitness instructor (male, single, deeply divine) and the party of five lesbians who spent all day hiking and all night playing folk songs on guitars. Susie didn't think much of the lesbians, who weren't the acceptable lipstick type, but the more earthy, hairy variety. Susie and hair, except on the head, were not friends. I managed to get in one question and a very important one—did they serve wine with dinner?

'Girls,' cried Susie, 'of course they serve wine with dinner!' I heard Rach heave a deep sigh of relief.

◌ Dinner with the dieters

I desperately tried to persuade Jules that we should dine out.

'Don't be silly, Rach. Susie's a bore but the others will be lovely. You'll see.'

'They so clearly won't be lovely I don't even know where to begin. Weren't you listening to that dreadful woman? This place is crawling with neurotics and hypochondriacs and we don't want to get to know any of them.'

'We've already paid for this meal.'

Pause.

'Fine,' I said, 'we'll eat here. But I'm not going to be pleasant. If I don't want to talk I'm going to claim a socio-psychological impediment, just like everyone else.'

'Attagirl! You'll have fun being annoying.'

'No, I won't.'

As it turned out, I didn't have to make an excuse not to talk, because no-one could get a word in around Susie and Jean. The two women had taken up tactical positions at opposite ends of the table and were engaged in recreating the Battle of Hastings. Susie had taken an early lead in the campaign with an opening manoeuvre designed to capture the allegiance of the populace—at the top of her voice, she was grilling Lucy the Juice Drinker on her weight problem.

'Eight weeks on the Soup Diet and not a pound shed!' bawled Susie, for the benefit of the rest of the guests who might not be up to speed on Lucy's problem. 'What are we going to do with you?'

Lucy reddened and looked around the table like a chastised puppy, hoping that her shameful secret hadn't travelled beyond her and Susie. It was a vain hope. Every face at the table was goggling at her sympathetically. Cunning Susie. Nothing like someone else's disastrous weight problem to grab people's attention.

'I . . . er . . .' Lucy looked around for an escape route but found her shoulders had been pinned into her chair by ten, acrylic, French polished nails. Susie had a valuable hostage and she wasn't letting her go.

'Have you tried the Israeli Army diet?' yelled Susie. 'Eggs for the first two days, apples for the second two days, salad for the third two days, and chicken, no skin of course, for the last two days. A stone in a week, I swear.'

Lucy tried turning to a higher authority for help. 'My dietician says it's best to shed the weight slowly.'

'Dietician!' Susie disposed of the higher authority with one shriek. 'You're wasting your time, darling. They always give you that claptrap about slow weight loss being permanent weight loss. That's how they make their money. No, your fat is here to stay. It's clinging on like a first wife. Surgery is what I'd recommend. Now I know a divine cosmetician who'll have that tummy tucked before you can say, 'Pass the whipped cream, I'm stapled!' You need to start thinking drastic, darling, and this man is a sweetie. He'll have you halved in a week.'

My heart went out to Lucy. She was gazing into Susie's face, helpless. All around her, thinner guests were making sympathetic noises and covertly eyeing her upper arms. Susie had them in the palm of her hand—the guests *and* the upper arms. In fact, Lucy was going to have to have cosmetic surgery on the marks Susie was leaving. While Lucy squirmed beneath her torturer, Susie regaled her and the rest of the table with tales of weight loss miracles she had personally observed in friends (some of them delightfully famous)—tummy tucking, bowel shortening, liposuction, aversion therapy. Nothing as dull as exercise, of course. Susie knew how to keep her audience transfixed. My heart stopped going out to Lucy—it was too busy going out to me. I gazed at Jules, helpless. How much more of this was I going to have to bear? Jules grimaced back at me. I had no idea what she was trying to convey, but probably some nonsense about being patient.

At the other end of the table, Jean was turning purple. She too was gazing at Susie, helpless, but for quite other reasons. So ferocious had Susie's initial onslaught been that Jean had found herself vanquished before the battle had even begun. Not two words had she managed to utter. She had tried to attack Susie head on by simply starting to talk and had got as far as 'I . . .' before being swamped by Susie's superior volume. She had tried to win over the population by raising her eyebrows and smiling wearily at other guests as if to say, 'Isn't this woman *awful?*', but her targets were too busy comparing themselves in secret relief to Lucy to respond to this cue. So Jean just had to wait, her only hope a war of attrition. Surely, sometime, Susie must start to weary.

It seemed as though even this tactic was to be proved useless when, about twenty minutes into Susie's campaign, the empty carafe diverted her attention. Unthinkingly, lulled perhaps by her military success, Susie shut her mouth and Jean trumpeted her forces into a surprise attack. She began by disguising herself as a partisan and commencing with a discussion of diet.

'I'm on the raw and parboiled vegetable diet for my arthritis and my eczema,' she announced to the table. 'I've got the worst eczema my doctors have ever seen.' All eyes turned to Jean. Susie was caught with a mouthful of wine. It was her turn to gaze, helpless. 'They didn't know what it was at first. They thought it was cancer and Alice (and here she turned to a shrivelled specimen sitting beside her) was ever so scared, weren't you Alice? We thought I'd have to go to hospital for an operation, like I did last year when I had my terrible fall and injured my back—ooh, they thought I'd never walk again, didn't they Alice? The doctors said they'd never seen anything like it on the x-ray. One young doctor told me that when he saw my x-ray he thought he was looking at a *quadriplegic* it was so bad.'

Jean had quickly revealed her battle plan. She wasn't going to compete with Susie using the weapons of famous friends and liposuction. No, Jean's strength lay in her many, many weaknesses. Her Magna Carta was the right of all free women and men to have an interesting illness.

'I have a kind of eczema that only three other people in the world have, or maybe it was three other people in the hospital, I forget. Anyway, it's *very rare*. They couldn't do anything for me, could they Alice? And then I had the most appalling headaches, and every bone in my body hurt. I never complained though, never said a word, did I Alice? But, oh, I was in agony, I can tell you. I had to go to one specialist after another and in the end, do you know what it was?'

I couldn't resist. 'Hypochondria?'

Jules choked on her wine.

Luckily, Jean seemed to suffer from deafness as well. 'Arthritis. Can you believe that? Arthritis at my age—who'd have believed it?'

Jules kicked me under the table, missed and hit the table leg.

'What did you say, dear?' said Jean.

'I said, oooooooww . . . of course not. Ridiculous.'

'Well, it's true. The doctors couldn't believe it, either. And I've got the worst kind, too. I've had cortisone injections, and I've had to cut out tomatoes and cheese, and cheese was my favourite food, wasn't it Alice? It seems so unfair that I have to give up my favourite food.' With all eyes on her and her command of the field secured, Jean burbled on happily.

Jules and I looked at each other in agony, although Jules was in slightly more agony since she'd given the table leg a fair whack. When was this going to end? The other diners at our table actually seemed interested. They were saying things like, 'Ooh, cortisone, I've had that, it's terribly hard on the system' and 'How brave of you' and 'Cancer, how awful!'

I couldn't believe it. I wanted to scream, 'Yes cancer is awful, IF YOU'VE HAD IT. Which she HASN'T.' Susie and Jean had made cunning conversational choices. Jules and I might be reeling but the rest of the table actually seemed to think that weight loss surgery and imaginary diseases made for enthralling listening.

To add to our misery, the only food available had apparently been labelled by medical staff. There was no menu, but there *was* a laminated list for each guest explaining the dietary codes. Blue dots meant vegetarian. Red dots meant low fat. Yellow dots meant wheat and gluten free. Pink meant yeast free. A plate with a red and a blue dot was a low fat, vegetarian dish. Jules pointed to one plate with all four coloured dots on it and whispered, 'Surely there can't be anything on that plate. It must be for the breatharians.' Which was quite funny, but not even that could cheer me up for long and my temper was fraying fast. I signalled to Jules that I wanted to run. *Now.* Jules signalled back: *Eat first.* I signalled back again: *And then we're going.* We were like two fifth columnists planning our escape from enemy territory.

Meanwhile, Susie had spotted a breach in her opponent's defences and was preparing to mount an offensive. She tapped her fingernails briskly against her glass.

'Heavens above, don't tell me you actually eat cheese? I haven't touched cheese in years. Don't you know how bad it is for you?' Susie gave Jean a look that managed to be horrified and smug at the same time.

Jean was immediately on the defensive, 'I've given it up! I've had to, because of my terrible arthritis. I told you that.'

'But are you sure it really is arthritis, darling—because eating too much cheese can cause symptoms just like it.'

Jean looked furious. 'Of course I have arthr . . .' She tried to counterattack but she had ceded vital tactical ground. Susie had the diners' attention—who eats *cheese* these days?

'You need to see a specialist, darling. Now I know a divine little man . . .' And she swiftly gathered the reins of power in her hands, determined not to let go this time.

As soon as we could, we escaped to the lounge, where everything had seemed so normal and pleasant when we first arrived. Had we made a terrible mistake coming to a health spa? It seemed more like the set of *One Flew Over the Cuckoo's Nest*. I said we should rip the drinks machine out of the wall and hurl it through the window, then we could leave the same way. Jules said only a couple of them seemed to be utterly awful. Perhaps the others would be all right when away from the influence of Susie and Jean. We uncorked one of the bottles Jules had smuggled from the dining room and prepared to get very, very drunk—when we noticed we weren't alone.

☞ 𝐘 Rach and Jules meet Folk Festival Girl

A pair of brown eyes was looking at us over the back of the armchair.

'Got a spare glass?'

'Sure.'

'It's awful, isn't it?' The owner of the brown eyes stood up and took a glass from Jules. She was wearing a brown suede fringed jacket and brown cowboy boots, so we assumed she must be one of the folk-singing lesbians. 'Cheers.'

'Cheers,' said Jules. 'Are they all like that?'

'Most of 'em.'

'We thought we'd be lying around getting massaged and pampered and letting our minds roam free, not trapped in a petrie dish of neurotics.'

'Wait until you try to get some evening air on the verandah. That's where all the smokers hang out.'

'There are smokers here?' Rach couldn't believe it. 'You can't get a steak, but you can light up a Winnie Blue?'

'Didn't you get a steak? You only have to ask at the kitchen. The food for those of us who eat is pretty good.'

'What about your friends?'

'Who?'

'Aren't you here with the les . . . I mean the . . .' Jules tried to find a politically correct way to describe a group of women who share a common sexual orientation without actually mentioning their defining characteristic.

The brown eyes twinkled at her. 'You mean the dykes? No, I've just come from the folk festival in Canberra. They were there, too, but I didn't meet them until I got here. I'm travelling solo.'

We were impressed. A girl travelling on her own. We hadn't had the guts to try that one.

'Don't you get lonely?'

'Well, I like my own company so, no, not very often. But I know what you mean. How do I walk into a restaurant alone? That sort of thing?'

We nodded. Jules said, 'I can't stand it when I see something great and I can't turn to the person next to me and talk about it.'

'Yeah, it has its drawbacks, but you just have to know where to go, like folk festivals. They're great. You take your tent and set up in a field full of campers and there you are, right in a really friendly neighbourhood. Everyone talks to everyone else and at night, when you're in your tent, you can hear people all around you. You get to have company at meal times and then peace at night. It's beautiful. I go all the time—to Canberra, and the one in Jamberoo. There's the Woodstock Folk Festival in Queensland, which is huge. It opens your eyes to new music, too. I got back home from my first one and went to a gig at the Tempe Hotel, where one of the bands was playing. All these people I'd met at the festival were there. It was like a school reunion, except everyone's really nice to each other.'

'We always travel together,' we said, and told her about the Holiday Buddy System.

'What's going to happen when one of you gets a boyfriend?'

We looked at each other. We'd never thought of that. It just seemed so unlikely. Rach said, '"When" I get a boyfriend. That's an interesting new concept.'

'I'll tell you why I'm asking. I used to have two Camping Buddies and we had a wonderful team going. We were all good at different things. I did the driving and washing up. Carmen did the cooking and booking the campsite, and Jason took care of the fire. That man could light a fire in the pouring rain with two wet sticks and no lighter. The best thing about it was the sense of having this special thing that was ours—our camping fraternity. I called us the Lucky Campers, because everything worked out so well for us— we always got a good spot, it never rained during the day and thanks to Jason, rain, hail or snow at night, we were never without a fire.

'Then Carmen and Jason fell in love and straight away things changed. The next trip I found myself camping not with two Camping Buddies, but with one Camping Couple.

They held hands and gazed into each other's eyes. If one went for a walk, the other had to go too. Almost more unbearable was their concern for me. "Are you all right?" they'd ask periodically, because they didn't want me to feel lonely. Yech! And it got worse. The next time I planned a trip, Carmen couldn't come. Normally, that would be okay, because Jase and I would go and we'd manage the cooking somehow. This time, though, Jase said to me, "Oh, if Carmen's not going, then I don't think I will." Jase learned to drive, so they could go away together without relying on me. It was the little things like that that hurt. The rearranging of their lives because I was no longer necessary, and worse, I was in the way. I vowed then and there never to rely on a buddy again.'

We looked thoughtful.

Why we need men

Of course that wasn't going to happen to us. Was it? Jules couldn't help thinking of her friend Trisha who had just hooked up with a man. Before Trisha used to be up for a film or a chick-chat any day; now she's designated Saturday as her free day and has informed Jules that she is available to see her then, but at no other time. As soon as Trisha got a partner, her single friends got sidelined. Trisha has a much more important relationship to attend to now.

We thought about this—it was horribly true. Why do single girls yearn for couplehood? It's so we'll have someone whose job it is to be the special person in our life. That's the thing that's missing. You can cobble together Claytons relationships like holiday buddies, or film-on-Saturday buddies, where you and your single girlfriend commit to each other for certain activities, but the fact is that you'll lose those relationships in a nanosecond if a man comes along. So what happens to the single girl who never gets a partner? How does she create a life that isn't going to fall apart on the arbitrary appearance of a man? Rach has almost given up hope.

Rach tries another way

It's true, you know. Especially after giving my number to that guy I really liked and never getting a return phone call. I was so sure we had a spark. And I was so wrong. How much more humiliation can I take? The answer is none. I can't take any more humiliation. I'm giving up. Seriously. I've been hanging around for fifteen years waiting for a guy I can talk to for the rest of my life to turn up, and he hasn't. Or if he has, he's carrying baggage way over the weight limit—I refer to my dear Byron's drunken misbehaviour. I loved Byron and I could talk to him all day, every day. But not on weekends, when he turned into someone I'd never met before, someone who poured himself around a bottle of scotch, then jabbered out a lot of tedious claptrap before setting off into the night in search of skirt. Oops, did that sound bitter? I'm not really bitter at all, too much time has passed.

But I am bitter about Liz, yes, LIZ, the next person I fell in love with. What sort of hilarious prank was God playing there? I swear, Liz is the only person I have fallen in love with on sight. She walked into the room, our eyes met, our gaze held, and the room was filled with sunshine. In my memory, I've added the sound of angels singing, but that didn't really happen. The sudden burst of sunlight happened though, truly.

But there was a slight hitch—I'm not gay. Liz was gay, so that was one problem taken care of, but I'm not. I'm not even a little bit gay. I'm 100 per cent hetero. I talked myself all through that one, desperate to find a way to stay with this wonderful woman, while going out to endless lunches with her and listening to every glorious, insightful, poetic word she said. In the end I decided that the only thing a hetero girl needs is a penis now and then, so if Liz would consent to the occasional use of a strap on, I reckoned I could do the gay thing. I'd have to learn to go down on a woman, but for her, I'd do it. Not a problem. I was just about to declare my love when I discovered that Liz already had a partner, and one she would never leave, so my heart quietly broke and I forgot about trying to be gay. But honestly—a woman? Did the cosmos get a good laugh out of that one?

One day, I decided that waiting for love is a mug's game. I thought I wanted children (I was young and naive at the time) so I came up with a cunning plan. My friend Kate, who's a struggling artist, wants a family. She'd been single for a fair while, so I suggested to her that we move in together, that she get pregnant using the donated sperm of a willing friend of ours, and that we have a few kids and live as a family. I'd be the breadwinner, because I'd rather do that than be the mother, and she could bring up the kids and pursue her art in more comfort than she does now.

I spent some months trying to convince her. I even found a sperm donor. I really wanted George Taxi, but George is funny about his sperm. He thinks that sex is how women suck the life out of men, and he'd prefer to hang on to his semen. So I asked around and got Leslie to agree. Leslie filled all our criteria—smart, good looking, happy nature. But still Kate wouldn't set up a family with me. Why not? Because she can't give up the idea that one day she'll find a male partner and get the family *and* the love and intimacy you get from a couple. It's a different and, we all secretly feel, a better love and intimacy to the sort you get from your friends.

⌐👓 ⍀ We contemplate the love of friends

Folk Festival Girl agreed with the last one. 'But you can't keep trying to pretend you have it. You have to embrace your singleness and really enjoy it or you waste your life in empty hope. That's why I started to travel alone. And you know what? It's scary at first, but then it's fun. You just don't see how very, very free you are when you're single. You only focus on how lonely you are. But there are a lot of advantages to the single life—you can sleep in whenever you want, you can go wherever you want, do whatever you want. There are plenty of women with four kids and a husband whose mother rules his life who'd swap with you tomorrow.'

'She gets sex, though, right, this woman with the kids and husband?' This from Jules, who's suffering from her very long, dry spell.

'Yeah, there is that.'

'Yeah.'

And we all looked thoughtful.

'It may not be great sex, of course.'

'No.'

'Or it may be. She has to have some compensation if she's got four kids.'

'That's how she got the four kids in the first place.'

'Another chardy, Rach?'

'Don't mind if I do, Jules.'

We reached for another bottle. What Folk Festival Girl had said made sense, and yet, somehow, we still didn't want to be single. We agreed, however, that we would never cravenly desert each other if the miracle should happen and one of us actually got to have sex again. We were very emphatic about this. We made a solemn vow and clinched it with red wine, because that looked more like blood than the chardy.

Then Jules told a story about the time she fell desperately in love with a lead singer of a boy band. She ditched all her friends, all her other interests, and became caught up in the life of a groupie until the day she found him with the rhythm guitarist of the same band, making music of the kind that is banned in some American states. When she protested, he told her to drop a mandy and join in, claiming his rights as an artist. She returned to her old life and her patiently waiting friends, who could have told her it would all end in tears, but who forebore to say I told you so.

Folk Festival Girl countered with a story from her dark past as a desperate single, when she had had an ill-advised liaison with a married man—what liaison with a married man is not ill-advised, you might well ask—which had ended when his wife became pregnant, and his protestations that it must have been someone else sounded thin even to his ears. She spent a month on her best friend's sofa, crying and being fed chocolate and hash cakes by the person who would stick by her through thick and thin. Love, she realised, wasn't to be found through passion, it was right there where you left it—in the arms of your best friend.

Then Jules sang a song about love that always makes her cry. It made us all cry so we had a group hug, and Folk Festival Girl said we needed to come face to face with our inner souls, so we cracked open another bottle and lay on the floor to get in touch with the Universal Goddess, a person Folk Festival Girl apparently knew quite well, from the way she talked about her. Unfortunately, something about lying on the floor gave us the giggles, so we stopped trying to reach our inner children and resumed swapping stories of staunch friendship. Rach fell asleep halfway through one of her stories and we had to wake her up to finish it. We may have started line dancing at one point, it's hard to say.

CHAPTER FOUR

The Joy of Bad Sex

♈ Jules is made of the right stuff

We had decided to sleep in our clothes on the floor of Folk Festival Girl's room. It's frightfully good for the posture, sleeping on the floor. And as for the clothes . . . well, never mind, we had our reasons no doubt. I can't say I felt in tip-top form, and Rach appeared to require urgent medical help—her eyelids were glued together. She seemed to think that since we were at a health retreat she may as well catch up on some much needed sleep—at least, that's how I chose to interpret her snarl when I tried to wake her up and get her off Folk Festival Girl's floor. Luckily, Folk Festival Girl didn't mind her room being turned into a doss house so we left Rach to her sleep therapy and got into our shorts and Ts for the bike hike.

I was determined to lose a bit of weight on this holiday. I'd had enough lying around feeling sorry for myself and nurturing a resort for fat cells on my stomach. It was time the fat found itself another host. I don't smoke and I'm a moderate drinker (don't give me that look) and I do a lot of walking, so I was expecting the bike hike to be a bit of a challenge, but nothing too disastrous. Really, I should have just stayed on the floor.

I had made a point of checking out this bike hike the previous night. It's not that I'm not fit, it's just that I could be fitter. Okay, I'm not fit. I want to exercise but I don't want to kill myself. So I asked the Team Leader—Physical Fitness, What grade is this hike? And he told me, easy to moderate. You're sure it's easy to moderate, I said. Yep, easy to moderate. No uphill marathons? No—a little hill at the end, but mostly flat. No rocky terrain? No, it's a nice easy road. Easy to moderate then. Yes, easy to moderate! His smile was starting to freeze so I left it at that. But you have to be sure, because if it's too hard it's just not fun.

Why did I bother asking? About six of us plus the Team Leader started out—me, Folk Festival Girl, three of the lesbians and Alice, the silent widow. For the first two minutes the ride was indeed, easy. We sailed along a bitumen road through rather pretty countryside, past grazing cattle and the occasional bounding kangaroo. The lesbians joked heartily with the Team Leader, challenged each other to races to the next road sign, and in general behaved like a bunch of hearty girl guides. Folk Festival Girl hummed a tune and gazed about her, and Silent Alice and I brought up the rear. I don't know what Alice was thinking about, but I was concentrating on keeping a nice steady rhythm going with my breathing. You want to pace yourself with exercise. No good throwing yourself into it too early.

I was proved right when the road took a steepish turn and we had to put a bit of legwork into getting ahead. The lesbians had thrown themselves a bit too heartily into their races and were beginning to labour. They weren't giving in, though; they put their all into conquering the hill with every appearance of enjoyment. Alice and I were going okay, but our silence was a bit grimmer and more determined than it had been a few minutes ago. Just when I was thinking I'd reached about the limit of my endurance the road took a turn to the right, and we were staring at an upward slope of about 90 degrees. We all groaned loudly, but the Team Leader gaily challenged us to see who could get to the top first and everyone but me set to. I gave the Team Leader a mildly filthy look and got off my bike to push. There's nothing of the A-type competitor about me. As far as I was concerned, I'd stopped having fun and I blamed the Team Leader who had lied to me so smoothly. This was not an 'easy to moderate' ride. Had I not made it perfectly clear what constituted an 'easy to moderate' rating? Had I not specifically requested a ride lacking hills of spirit-breaking steepness? In a just world, my lawyers would have had something to say to this used-car salesman of a Team Leader, something about the laws of fair trading and truth in advertising. I wondered if Rach was still on the floor—smart woman, that Rach. She doesn't get easily persuaded by fads of the moment, like exercise and diet, just does her own thing. There should be more of it.

Silent Alice had a bash at pedalling up but, after about twenty seconds, she thought the better of it and joined me on foot as we gently steered our bikes up the hill, taking time out every now and then to stop and smell the flowers. The others were waiting for us at the top, and joked and laughed about our slowness. 'We'll have to work on your fitness, you two. A little slope like that, and you have to walk it!' Never mind, they'd found a nice diversion while they were waiting for us—a bush track which left the road at the top of the hill. Would we like to ride the track to see an aboriginal cave painting? It was a very easy ride, but the track was dirt, so the Team Leader had told them. The Team Leader was very bright and chirpy, the scoundrel. I said No, I thought I'd stay here and enjoy the view, but Alice said Yes (the first word I'd heard out of her the entire stay), and so off the lot of them went down the track, while I enjoyed a peaceful commune with Nature, who was at her Australian best—sun shining, fragrant breeze ruffling the hair, bush on one side, fields on the other, cows and horses looking brown-eyed and content. I'm not one for hanging onto my grudges and it only took five minutes of this treatment to soothe the savage beast. I sat on a rock and practised my meditation, which I was getting rather good at. So good in fact that I didn't even realise that 40 minutes had passed before the others returned.

They were not looking as bouncy on their return. In fact, the lesbians were looking positively sullen. Folk Festival Girl whispered to me that I had made the right decision. The track was pretty much boulders all the way down and they'd ended up carrying their bikes most of the way there and back. The Team Leader made a couple of tentative jokes, trying to re-capture the spirit of the start of the ride, but the look in the eye of the biggest and toughest of the lesbians stopped him cold and we rode on in silence. The road was tarmac from there but after coasting down gently for a while the road began to rise, and then to rise a little more. By now it was midday and the sun was beating down pretty sternly. I am a redhead, so I had a hat because I can't step out my front door without bathing in suncream and donning a burkah, but the others were starting to look a bit pink on the neck and face. Hard to tell if it was sun or anger that caused the redness—probably an unhappy combination of both. Riding at the head of the pack, the Team Leader slowed down and came to a halt at a rough-looking turn off. He turned around as we all trundled up to him, and he seemed just a little hesitant.

'Well now, hehehe, we have to go off road here, hehehe. Just a little bush track to take us back to the resort and a lovely shower before lunch. Now I won't lie to you . . .'

Someone let out a low growl.

'. . . it's a bit rough, but nothing you can't handle, just a little bit of dirt and a few stones. Hehehe, you'll be able to eat all you like after a workout like this. That'll be nice, won't it?'

Poor sap. He was trying so hard and getting it so wrong. Lesbians don't care about calories, at least not the ones who have renounced high heels and razor blades and who recognise a mechanism for social control when they see one. The tough one looked like she was winding up to give him a lecture on The Perils of Patronising Women followed by an uppercut to the jaw. Folk Festival Girl and I exchanged a little grin and, because she is a kind-hearted girl, she gave him a helping hand.

'How long does it take to ride the track?'

His gratitude was palpable.

'Oh minutes! Hardly any time at all. Really, no more than ten minutes. At the most, fifteen minutes. We'll be home before you know it. Come on then girls, let's see who can get home first!' And we slowly wheeled our bikes onto the dirt track for the last leg of our journey.

What was the story with this Team Leader? Did he have some illness that prevented him from ever telling the truth? He was in the wrong business. His father should have sat him on his knee when still a lad and said, 'Son, there's only one profession that will reward a tongue as forked as yours, and a character as false—politics. Or possibly law. Make one of these your career and you will flourish and multiply.' And when his son said to him, 'Daddy, I've decided to become a sports therapist,' his father should have told him that the healing sciences generally require the practitioner to be on nodding terms with fact and truth.

We were not ten minutes from home. We were not even twenty minutes from home. We might have been twenty minutes from home if the track had indeed been 'dirt with a few stones' but it wasn't. It was rocks and boulders with a bit of dirt thrown on top. It was ruts and potholes and fallen trees, and I was surprised we didn't see the skeletons of previous bike hikers by the side of the track where they'd fallen, wearied beyond endurance.

Fifty minutes at least, it took us, and they were

50 gruelling, sweaty, lung-searing minutes in the middle of a blazing Australian day. We were all in a filthy mood. The sun shone down on us and we cursed it bitterly. Birds twittered and we told them to put a sock in it. The Team Leader was behaving like a boy whose mother had caught him stealing from the biscuit tin and who was now trying to be very, very quiet in the hope she'd forget about his existence, not to mention his crime, by the time Dad got home to administer the hiding. By the time we reached the retreat we were too exhausted to give him the punishment he so richly deserved. I headed straight back to my room for a long, long shower and poured out this sorry tale to Rach, begging her to stop me should I ever contemplate a bike ride again.

⌒🍸 Rach and Jules indulge themselves

Well, of course we weren't going to put up with that sort of treatment. After Rach had stopped laughing (she's got a black sense of humour), we decided to spend the rest of our time here indulging ourselves in every decadent activity the place offered. Rach had crawled out of Folk Festival Girl's room and straight into the hydro-bath which she now highly recommended to Jules.

'You lie in a huge warm bath for an hour while mighty jets of water spray up and down your body under the surface. It's great! Word of warning—go to the loo first. If you get stuck in the hydro-bath and your bladder starts giving little hints, the rushing water becomes less soothing and more of a cunning torture the Chinese might have thought up. I didn't want to leave in the middle of my treatment, but I had to— it was just too painful. I was a bit worried that other hydro-bathers may have taken the other option, but the Duty Nurse, or whatever she was, assured me that the bath water is changed for every treatment.'

Jules took her up on the hydro-bath challenge and followed it up with the Head, Neck and Shoulders massage with manicure and pedicure. We were both starting to feel really good, and even Rach agreed that the money had been well spent. Jules had the added pleasure of feeling virtuous as well, and began to bore on and on about how great it feels when you've really given your body a good work out, really worked up a sweat and put yourself to the test. She thought we might head off to the mountains after our stay here and climb some peaks, really get fit while we were away. Rach reminded her that the retreat offered spin classes and there was one on at five pm she might like to attend and that shut her up.

Instead of the spin class, we took a yoga class and finished off the day with a champagne in the spa. Folk Festival Girl, who'd done the meditation class and a spiritual healing session, joined us and took a glass of champers to get in touch with her alcoholic side. She told us that a group from the retreat was going to the local pub to have dinner and check out the action. We love a pub meal and, with the memory of last night's dinner companions still seared in our brains, we agreed to meet her there.

We dine à la pub

The local was a typical country pub with a juke box and pool tables, the darts competition stats chalked up next to the darts board and a meat raffle on Saturdays. This was a Thursday and the place was full, but not jam-packed. Just pleasantly loud and crowded enough to let you melt into the atmosphere and relax. We spotted Folk Festival Girl by the pool table, chalking her cue and looking surprisingly intense as she studied the position of the balls, her head a little to one side and one eye slightly narrowed. Obviously a girl who takes her pool seriously. Two of the lesbian folk singers were there as well, talking, watching the table and generally settling in for a convivial evening.

Jules pointed out the Team Leader—Physical Fitness standing at the bar, buying a round. He was quite a good-looking fellow, really rather attractive when seen from behind. Jules remembered now that she'd noticed this aspect of him when she'd seen him in his bicycle shorts earlier.

'It's when he opens his mouth that disappointment sets in.'

We contemplated the view for a couple more seconds.

'We've really got to have sex soon.'

Long pause.

'Okay, enough of this, let's get to know the girls.'

The girls were Jen and Carol, a couple in their late fifties. Carol was the tough one—she'd spoken her mind to the Team Leader after the disastrous bike ride, poor guy—but she turned out to be not so much tough as sure of herself. Someone who had seen enough of life with the clear eyes of the outsider to know without a shadow of a doubt where she stood and what she thought. She had a way of summing you up with her eyes that made you feel she was looking straight into your naked soul. Jen was less confronting. She had big, round, baby-blue eyes in a little girl face that said 'Please love me'. Her face somehow didn't quite match her body which was the squat, square-handed body of an ex-nurse accustomed to lifting semi-conscious bodies off chamber pots. Jen was a chatter, a maker of small talk, and she set about telling us the story of her life with only the tiniest encouragement from the affable Jules.

It turned out that Jen and Carol both had grown-up kids, both had married early in an era when telling your parents you're a lesbian was a bit more problematic than it is now, and both had left their husbands when they met each other and fell in love. It hadn't been easy on anyone—husbands, kids or Jen and Carol—and in the end, after marriage counselling and psychotherapy, after crying, confused kids, and shouting, angry husbands, they'd turned their backs on the lot of them and started a new life in the country. They bought a run-down hotel and joined the local Gay and Lesbian Support Group. At first, the hotel had catered to anyone who was kind enough to drop in. But soon, as their social circle expanded, their clientele became more specific. It's like that in the gay and lesbian community—they support one another. Before they knew it, Jen and Carol had a thriving, orientation-specific business, a Lesbian Only Hostel.

Lesbian hostels—who knew?

'I wish I were gay.' (Rach, in case you couldn't guess.) 'You'd get to marry your best friend, and then you'd have this whole community supporting you *and* your business. Why isn't there a single women's network like that? We should have a network of Hetero Hostels for Single Chicks.'

'We're trying to find the perfect holiday for a single girl,' said Jules. 'Somewhere you can go where you don't stand out like a . . . like a . . . well like a lonely singlette in a sea of hand-holding couples.' They're not crash hot on similes in the public service, but Jules' indignation finished her sentence for her.

Folk Festival Girl looked up from her cue, 'I've been telling them about the music festival scene.'

'Yeah, that's a good one. That's top of our list so far. Somewhere you can go alone and be totally at ease. We're looking for places like that.'

'You can stay at our hostel.' Jen was delighted to give a couple of strangers something that would make them happy.

'We're not gay.' Wasn't that obvious? Rach can't stop going on about it.

'That doesn't matter. We love having straight women stay at the hostel.'

'But isn't there the same "couple" problem? I'm not sure it's any different being alone in a sea of same-sex couples.'

'We're all women, so it is different. No-one is left out if they need company. It's like that at all the gay and lesbian hostels.'

'But don't the gay guests mind having hetero women around?'

'Gay women like straight women.'

'What do you mean by like, exactly?'

Carol grinned. Jen was looking a bit hurt because she really wanted us to be excited that we'd found a new single chick heaven, and we were spoiling it by joking about it. Then she saw Carol's face and she decided to be roguish instead.

'Well you might get a few looks . . .'

'Really??'

Jules rolled her eyes. 'Oh lordy! I'm getting another drink. What can I get you all?' She took the drinks orders and Rach settled down to discuss her incipient (and utterly imaginary) lesbian tendencies with the experts.

◑ᴠ Rach skips the boring bits, then rescues a fallen friend

You don't want to hear the whole discussion, I'm sure. I had a long and intimate conversation with the sympathetic Jen on sexuality (mostly mine) and anxiety disorders (mostly hers). I told her about my disturbing experience falling in love with a woman and my confusion about whether or not I was gay—how does one know? Jen told me in gory detail the story of her disastrous marriage, how she'd known from puberty that she was attracted to women, and how she'd been forced to suppress her true self. I've often wondered if I'm suppressing my true self, although I suspect when I get onto some subjects my friends wish I'd suppress my true self a bit more.

Carol didn't say much but she had my number. The test of a lesbian is simple—do you go down on other women? If you don't, you ain't. I, as I've said earlier, don't; so I ain't, and Carol knew it. But Jen was enjoying herself, so Carol was indulgent, and refrained from telling me to get a life.

We'd moved onto the interesting topic of Jen's emotional disorders and precisely how they'd displayed themselves before the helpful intervention of medical science and pharmaceutical companies, when Carol broke into the conversation.

'Isn't that your friend kissing Sam?'

'Who?'

'Sam, the physical fitness instructor from the retreat.'

I looked over at the bar and saw, to my horror, that Jules was indeed locked in an embrace with the nice-bottomed Team Leader—or 'Sam', as I supposed we would have to call him after the marriage.

The only possible explanation was an alcohol overdose. Jules is suffering from the most terrible drought, poor girl. She's had no sex at all, apart from a disastrous one-night stand, for two years. Two years! It's enough to drive anyone mad and Jules is a woman who likes pleasures of the flesh— sex, eating, drinking. Especially drinking. She has a tendency to let her animal self out of its cage when she's had a few— it's all those years in the public service, suppressing her true self. Right now her animal self was behaving like a starving lion that's found a half-dead gazelle and is too hungry to bother killing it before hoeing in for the meal of a lifetime. I must say it was only by inference that I knew it was the

Team Leader she had in the stranglehold—I couldn't see his face but I recognised the bot.

Jules needed rescuing, but of course she wouldn't agree with me in her current state. How to separate her without a crow bar? Too easy for the seasoned professional—feign illness and demand to be taken home straight away. That's why hypochondriacs rule the world. No one can say 'no' to the sick. I tried to look as green as possible and tapped her on the shoulder.

'Mmmmmgggrrrmphhhh.'

'Jules, I feel terrible. We have to go.'

'Mmmmmgggrrphhh.'

'Jules!'

'Gggrrrrrrrrrr.'

'Jules!'

She came up for air and looked over her shoulder, still clutching her prey. 'Oh, for God's sake, can't you see I'm busy!'

'Jules, I feel faint. I don't think I can make it on my own.' I looked piteously at the Team Leader, who buckled, as I knew he would.

'That's okay, baby. Take her home and I'll meet you back at the retreat—say in the lounge? Eleven o'clock?'

Jules glared at me, realised she was defeated, then swung around and gave him a melting look, 'See you back there. Don't be late.'

It's a miracle I wasn't really sick right then and there.

'What is your problem?' Jules was understandably upset as I steered her towards the door. 'I finally get some action and you come barging in and mess it up. Can't you see I'm on a roll here?'

I opened the door and pushed Jules through it into the night.

'Right. You and the Team Leader—Physical Fitness are getting it on.'

Jules gasped as the cold air thwhacked her in the face. She stumbled forward, crashed into a lamp post, and clutched it with both hands as her legs gave way. At this late hour, her senses finally made an appearance.

'Rach. You saved me.'

'You betcha.'

'I was about to sleep with a man I despise.'

'Yup.'

'You remember the French Farce?'

'Vividly.'

'I almost did it again. You saved me.' She transferred her grasp from the lamp post to my arm and we started for home.

'I know,' said Rach. 'You owe me big. Did the French Farce teach you nothing?'

🍸 The French Farce—Jules' morality tale

The story of my affair (yes, yes, one-night stand) with a young French hunk is not one I tell easily, so it's a lucky thing I've had a couple of drinks.

I used to go to a certain coffee shop every day before work for a ritual cappuccino and a quiet read of the newspaper to get on top of current affairs for the day. One day, a new waiter served me. I gave him my instructions on the precise way to create my morning coffee—strong, not too much froth, one sugar (white), full cream milk—and he delivered one perfect cap to my table. The next day, I asked for a coffee and got perfection again. After that, every morning he simply produced exactly what I needed and put it in front of me without even taking my order. To my surprise, he seemed anxious to impress as well. His eyes lit up when he saw me and he cleaned tables with that extra bit of self-conscious grace one uses when someone we like is around. I was really rather chuffed, because I was about to turn 37, so any youthful admiration was a balm to the soul. We exchanged a few words now and then and I found out that he was French, a student and had rather scrummy brown eyes. I never discovered his name, but I took to thinking of him as 'Pierre'. About six weeks after he'd made that first, perfect cappucino, he told me that he would soon be leaving to take up a post elsewhere, something more in line with his studies. I never got very clear on what that was because his English was terrible, but I was quite clear on one thing. Shortly he would be gone. I wondered if he would get up the courage to ask me out.

Finally, his last day came. On that day, I finished my coffee and paper and went up to the counter with my bill, timing my approach so that my friend, and not one of the other waiters, would be the one I paid. You see, I had decided that if he didn't make a move, I was going to. Before leaving home I had written my name (first name only) and my phone number on a small piece of paper. This I now folded and placed under the exact change for the coffee. I pressed the lot into 'Pierre's' hand, paper at the bottom of the pile, and said, 'Well, goodbye. Good luck in your new job. Perhaps we'll meet again,' gave him a very warm smile and walked out. I felt so cool. I'd just given my phone number to a man whose name I didn't even know! But what the hey—I hadn't met anyone I liked in ages, it was January, the start of new things, and I just needed to do something for the hell of it.

I didn't know what would happen but to my surprise, he called that very night.

°Ello? Zjules? Zis is Pierre. From ze coffee shop. You give me your number.'

Yes, his name really was Pierre. Can you believe that? Was this fate or what? Now, I don't know what I had in mind—oh wait, yes I do—I had in mind a delightful romantic affair with a much younger man that might last a few months, maybe a year while he was here studying. A sophisticated, European experience whispering sweet French nothings to a gorgeous young man with delicious eyes. That's what I had in mind. Pierre, I was soon to discover, had quite another experience in mind. He began the conversation thus.

'So. Who is zis woman who gives me 'er phone number?' A tad roguish, but I put it down to shyness, or unfamiliarity with the English language. I've never been one for roguishness in men, or any other affectation. I remember one fellow who had a disastrous predilection for baby talk, who, as he dressed for dinner, told me he was making himself 'boo-ful' for me. I can't quite recall, but I believe they were the last words he ever spoke to me.

'Well, I work in an office in the inner city.' I presented the straight bat to Pierre, just in case roguishness was what he had in mind. He took the hint and our next few sentences were more straightforward—how long was he in Australia for? (A year, been here three months.) Where was he going with his new job? (Unintelligible.) How old was he? (Twenty-four. Ahem. I didn't actually ask him, it just happened to come up in conversation, so I didn't have to reciprocate.) He made sure to tell me that he lived for the day, he was 'easy come easy go', which I took to mean he was looking for an affair, not a relationship, and that was fine by me. It turned out that he lived around the corner from me, and I had begun to visualise a summer spent skipping over to Pierre's place for a foreign film and long, luxurious afternoon sex, when he said, 'I sink you should come over rrrright now.'

Right now? That was moving a bit fast, even for an affair. I thought maybe coffee on the weekend, and said so.

'Oh no, come over 'ere now. I want to see you.'

I had work the next day, so I wasn't too keen on going out, but just as I caught that thought I said to myself, 'Oh, please Jules, would you live a little?' and got his address.

Now, it's a while since I'd been to a young man's place and this one was appealingly furnished with second-hand couches and wooden plank bookshelves. Really very touching. He made me a gorgeous coffee the French way—very strong and black in tiny coffee cups—and then he jumped me. There's no other word for it. He leapt on me. I laughed a bit to cover up my surprise and held my hands to his chest to prevent him swooping in for a kiss. Straining against my hands, he gazed hungrily into my eyes and said, 'Women, zey are ze masters. Men, we are your slaves.'

Oh dear. Conflicting emotions arose in my breast. You see, he really was very attractive, and it had been a very long time, so when my body found itself in the arms of a very lovely and ardent Frenchman, it sprang to life and rolled up its sleeves ready for action. But my mind recoiled. Could I really sleep with anyone this corny? Yes, yes, for God's sake, yes, screamed my body. And I was just about to give in to its demands when he said, 'So, who is zis woman who gives me 'er phone number?'

Oh Christ! If he'd just keep his mouth shut I could get to have sex. What was I going to do? I know—shut it for him. So I let him kiss me—but that only went halfway to solving the problem because he was a terrible kisser, which, frankly, is a criminal fault for a soi-disant Lothario to have. How can you be 24 and not know how to kiss? His idea of a good kiss was to stick his tongue in my mouth as far as it would go and move it around frantically. Bzzzzzzzzzzzt! Wrong! You have to start gently . . . Oh God, I'm not going to give tutorials here—you know what I mean. So you'd figure I'd just get out of there, but unfortunately while clutching me and gazing deep into my eyes he'd managed to get my dress off and we were now skin to skin. Well, a girl's only human. I figured if I didn't get over my ridiculous requirement for brain and style to accompany body I was never going to have sex again. So I slept with him. And he was so crap at it that I never even came. It takes real skill to sleep with a sex-starved woman who is in a year-long dry spell and fail to make her come. If he'd have just stayed still and let me do the manoeuvring, we'd have had lift off. But no, he had to show me all his tricks. Bzzzzzzt, again. And he had to repeat, ad nauseam, 'Women are ze masters, men zey are zeir slaves.'

Oh well. I wrote that one off to bitter experience and went home. The end of the story is that, to my astonishment, Pierre called and called and called. I went overseas for three months, and when I came back, who was the first person on my phone? Pierre—would I come ovair? 'E would love to see me. No, I don't think so, Pierre. Goodbye. And I put the phone down with an air of finality even the budding Lothario couldn't ignore.

The moral of this story is don't let the romance of youth and European-ness fool you into thinking the sex will be any good. Or, if he's a terrible kisser, get out straight away. Or, your mind will not let your body have a good time if it's too affronted by his banality. Or perhaps the moral of the story is—could I have decent sex *soon*, please?! This drought is killing me.

CHAPTER FIVE

Our nation's capital

We make a quick getaway

The next morning we woke at the crack of dawn, because we'd forgotten to close the curtains when we got in last night. We both groaned, neither of us being what you might call morning people, and Jules groaned a bit more forcefully when she realised the ache in her head wasn't a dream. Then a bit more forcefully still when she recalled her narrow escape.

'Oh God, you saved me.'

'Not a problem, little buddy.'

'When will I learn?'

'Ah, Grasshopper. When the spring birds fly to their southern nests, then the light comes.'

'Ah, Old Geezer. Shut up.'

'Ah, Grasshopper, 40 lines for that: "I must not drink Jim Beam and kiss strange men."'

'Ohhhhhhhhhh,' from under the bedclothes, then, 'Oh my God, I'll have to see him today.'

Sound of unsympathetic laughter from Rach's bed.

'It's not funny. We're supposed to be on holiday. I'm supposed to be getting fit, relaxing, getting healthy. Look at me! This place is turning me into an alcoholic. This is the second morning I've woken up feeling like I've done ten rounds with Mike Tyson and now I have to slink around avoiding that ghastly little man. Oh God, what was I thinking?'

'Yes, what were you thinking?'

'I was thinking, Gee, this guy looks like Colin Firth and he has the charm, brains and personality to match the face. I think this might be love. This is love, this is the one, just call me MRS TEAM LEADER—PHYSICAL FITNESS.'

'Really?'

'Alcohol does that to you.'

'Coupled with your record-breaking drought.'

'Thank you. All helpful comments can go in the suggestion box.'

'We don't have to stay if you really don't want to, although I was kinda looking forward to breakfast with Jean. I'm dying to ask her about her allergies.'

'She didn't say anything about allergies, did she?'

'No, she didn't, but I'm betting she can't resist having allergies. I thought I'd find out how many she's got. And get her to name them. Possibly in alphabetic order. Or by the year in which she acquired them from first to most recent. Or in order of their discovery by medical science.'

'No, let's go. You can write to her from Canberra. I can't face another day here. I want to hit the road.'

'What, now?'

'Can we?'

'I haven't had coffee yet.'

'We can get it on the road.'

'But we've paid for breakfast!' Rach really hates wasting money.

'I'll buy you breakfast at McDonald's. C'mon, it'll be fun. The sun's only just up. We can drive through the countryside in the early morning dew.'

Long pause while we considered this option.

'All right,' said Rach. 'Let's do it.'

So we did a super quick pack, and snuck out of the place, keeping an eye and ear out for the Team Leader—Physical Fitness, just in case he was still in the lounge waiting for Jules.

⌔ On the road again

Once out on the open road we put on 'Dancing Queen' as loudly as Jules could stand it and settled into the drive to Canberra. Australia is magic at any time, but the countryside in the early morning is unbeatable. That's when the fauna are bounding about looking cute and exotic—we saw kangaroos and an emu going for a morning run by the roadside, and even spotted a wombat lumbering incredibly slowly off the road. The sight of all this glory had its effect on Jules and her bounce started to return, even if her head remained a bit jackhammered.

'Isn't this marvellous?' she said. 'I do love Australia.'

'Yeah.'

'It's the sight of cows and horses that does it for me the most. Farm animals grazing peacefully in the fields, acres and acres of open space. It's soul food.'

'Hey Jules, do you know if the Americans ever caught the anthrax killer?'

'No, I don't think they did.'

'Huh. I bet it was a woman. A man with a grudge turns up with an AK47, but a woman posts you anthrax.'

'What made you think of that?' asked Jules.

Pause.

'I don't know.'

We drove on, taking in the scenery.

'You know, Rach, I think we should go to the Snowy Mountains and do some mountain climbing.'

'Mm hmm.'

'No, really. It'd be good for us. We can join a hiking tour and stretch ourselves, get to know the fit under the fat. That's what being on holiday is all about. We'll get back to Sydney fit and muscular and then it'll be easy to keep going. It's hard going to the gym when you're in lousy shape and tired out from a day at work but if we push ourselves now, while we're relaxed and have plenty of time, then it'll be easy when we get back to normal.'

'Uh huh.'

'Are you listening to me?

'Yes—rock climbing, good for us, now or never.'

'Not rock climbing, hiking through the mountains. We can work on our quads while taking in the scenery, so much better than watching telly at the gym. Ooh, look, a winery—I wonder if they're open this early.'

Rach contemplates the role of exercise

I wasn't listening of course. I've heard all of this before, and so will you by the time we've finished telling you our story. Jules is convinced she's just one step away from having a fit, slim, tanned body for the rest of her life. No exercise fad is too ludicrous for Jules: she's done Pilates and yoga (four different schools); she's been on boot camp (looked terrific for three weeks, then the early mornings defeated her); she's had a fitness coach (slept with him); a Jane Fonda video; and she's even bought the Abdominator off the telly. If it costs a lot of money and *New Idea* reports that starlets are doing it, Jules will give it a go. She's always the first to leap enthusiastically into the latest fitness miracle, and she's always the first to subside. She never gives up though, she just finds that work has got very busy, or her sister's kids need looking after because the whole family has come down with measles, or she reads that running is bad for your knees, or the Abdominator breaks. She has a house full of barely used exercise gear—running shoes, rackets, medicine balls, wetsuits, walking machines, videos, books and wall charts. Jules thinks that fitness helps your state of mind. I say that's fine, but what about the state of your living room?

I, on the other hand, although riddled with faults as my closest friends will tell you, have no illusions when it comes to exercise. It's out. The closest I come to working on my body for the sake of my mind is having a Radox bath and lighting my Magnanimity Candle—magnanimity being, according to the wrapper, the virtue that heals the world. It's also a virtue at which I need considerable practice. So, following the instructions, I take the candle and I place it in a sacred space that honours me. As I light it I say the word 'Magnanimity' and allow it to resound through my mind and body. I repeat the word, breathe deeply and inhale the aroma, letting the candlelight illuminate my heart with the virtue of magnanimity . . . Nope, still a bitch. What can you do? But the bath is lovely.

George Taxi and Jules did once pester me into getting fitter. George is a complete lunatic on the subject of physical exercise, as he is on so many subjects. When Jules was in her boot camp phase she came as close to George's way of thinking regarding exercise as anyone is likely to. I'd started to put on a bit of weight and I made the mistake of complaining about it to George and Jules, who quite rightly told me to put up or shut up. I didn't want a middle-aged spread so I put myself in their hands. They both thought that shock therapy was the only thing which would have any effect on a blob like me, so they signed me up for boot camp. Oh dear.

First, boot camp, for those of you who don't know about it, is the latest corporate craze. You get all dressed up in khaki, form two lines, and fitness instructors pretending to be drill sergeants yell at you while you do 100 push-ups, then run you up and down the steepest hill they can find in the CBD, shouting rude things about your body/motivation/

discipline. All this takes place at six o'clock in the morning. Why, I don't know. Presumably just to add to the pain. And 'No pain, no gain' is, of course, their motto. George and Jules signed me up for a two-week intensive.

I arrived at the gym at 5.45 in the morning, bleary eyed from lack of sleep and slightly out of breath from the walk up the stairs. I was the oldest and least fit of the group. All the rest were keen young corporate bunnies, full of vigour and the drive to be the very best they could possibly be at every moment of the live-long day. It tired me out just being in their peppy presence. After donning the regulation khaki t-shirt, we were hustled into line by a shouting fitness instructor, who told us that we were to address him as 'Sergeant' and his assistant as 'Corporal'. Very amusingly, his sidekick was less of an actor than perhaps the part required because he looked a bit startled and before he could stop himself he said, 'Oh, I thought *I* was the sergeant and you were the corporal. Aren't corporals the higher rank?' The 'sergeant' was momentarily thrown. Had he got it wrong? Then he pulled himself together. If *he* didn't know, then *we* wouldn't either. 'No,' he said firmly, 'I'm the sergeant and you're the corporal.' He continued on with the rules: We would follow instructions. When he asked us a question we would say 'Yes, sir' or 'No, sir'. We would not talk amongst ourselves. Anyone found slacking off would be punished with ten extra push-ups, '. . . and that won't be for you, that will be for the whole team, so look around you. Are you going to look after your mates? Or are you going let your team down?'

Well, I could have told him my answer right then and there. I'd never met these people before, so I couldn't give a bugger about my 'mates'. No point appealing to the team player in me—I'm on a team of one, buddy. But I held my tongue. No need to call attention to myself before we even began. Having completed his diatribe he ordered us to 'Riiiiiiight FACE!' and we began with a warm-up run to the park. After ten minutes I was so far behind the rest I'd lost sight of them. The 'corporal' stuck to my heels like a kindly terrier that's been told to nip the recalcitrant sheep and never mind their bleating and soft brown eyes. He shouted encouraging words into my ear, but I barely heard them through the crushing roar of my breathing. I sounded like an old man with emphysema who's just seen the Ghost of Christmas Past in the rec room and is trying to recover from the shock. Come to think of it, that's how I felt, too. I slowed to a walk just once, and the terrier started a high-pitched yapping. Walking was a sin, apparently. When we caught up to the others, who were just completing a second turn around the oval, the corporal reported my crime to the sergeant and the team was informed that ten extra push-ups would be added at the end of the session, thanks to 'someone' walking. Let that be a warning to you—we are serious.

There are some challenges I'm willing to take up and the spurious tough guy act is one of them. Memories of school and power-crazed house masters putting me on detention for daydreaming came flooding back. I reasoned thus: we are not really in the army; these people are corporate types who have important appointments at eight am; the gym staff cannot possibly keep us over the allotted time slot or they'll piss off their primary clientele; ergo, if I rack up enough push ups I can force the 'sergeant' into an awkward corner.

So I ran as long as I could, and when I needed to I walked. The terrier yapped; I ignored him. At the end of the session, I had clocked up 210 push-ups for my 'mates', and sure enough the sergeant had to quickly come up with a way of letting us go without letting us off the hook. Thinking fast, he made us do twenty of the extra push-ups and put the rest on to the end of the two weeks. I guess he figured he could use the whole last session to work off my punishments if I really pushed the point. And I fully intended to push the point but the next morning I woke up at five am, switched off the alarm and went back to sleep. Somehow, I never made it to another session. I wonder what happened to the 190 push-ups?

Having failed boot camp, George decided to take control of my exercise routine. He realised that I needed motivation, so every day George would ring me up at work and shout 'WHAT ARE YOU???' and I would reply, 'I'm a disgusting blob!'

'LOUDER!! WHAT ARE YOU???'

'I'M A DISGUSTING BLOB!'

'Is everything all right in there, Rach?' My supervisor put her head around the door.

'Fine thanks, Mary. I'm being motivated.'

'Oh, right.'

Then on Saturdays and Sundays before he started his shift, George Taxi made me run around Centennial Park. He spurred me on by playing the drill sergeant—a Hungarian Jewish drill sergeant, just for amusement's sake. He had the whole drill thing down, too. Here it is—you have to sing this to the tune of 'Sound Off' in a heavy Hungarian accent if you want the authentic experience:

Vun, two, sree, four

Find a man by Yom Kippur!

Five, six, seven, eight

A plastic surgeon vould be great!

DEN-tist!

(den-tist!)

DOC-tor!

(doc-tor!)

Or-tho-don-tist!

Law-yah!

ALL GOOD!

I can't run and laugh at the same time, so eventually I just gave up and let my waistline do whatever it thought best. Anyway, George is no better than Jules for sticking to fitness regimens. Like Jules, there's always a good reason why he's fallen off the wagon, usually because the tax office has caught up with him and he has to work extra shifts just to stay out of jail.

The tax office is always threatening to throw George in jail. It's the BAS thingy he finds so hard to manage. The poor guy spends nights wrestling it to the floor but it does no good—he's always months late. Then he has to work extra shifts to make the penalty payments which makes him fall behind on his taxes again, and so it goes on. The tax office seems to like threatening the defenceless souls who can't get on top of their paperwork. The government representatives who ring George from time to time can't seem to understand that he is a taxi driver, a sportsman and an artist—not a bookkeeper. Taxi drivers are romantic souls; they are wild and free; they roam the dark and smoky streets by night. They do not complete form A then go to question 6 if applicable.

George thinks fitness is the key to conquering depression, which he and I both suffer from. Once, when we were both too unhappy to get out of bed, George came up with an idea for incorporating our exercise regimen into our daily life. He called it the Salute to the Sun for the Terminally Depressed.

> *Morning Salute to the Sun—Perform Upon Awakening*
> Breathing in, open your eyes. Breathing out, gently stretch your legs. Breathing in, arise from your bed. Breathing out, lie on the floor sobbing. Breathing in, turn your face to the wall. Breathing out, execute the 1000-yard stare and contemplate the futility of exist-ence. Breathing in, crawl to the coffee machine. Breath-ing out, extend your arm and open the fridge. Breathing in, dispose of the month-old milk. Breathing out, commence the long march across the bleak tundra of your day.

I laughed so much I started to get happy again, and managed to get out of bed. I figure, why exercise to keep myself in a good frame of mind, when I can just ring George?

So I let Jules babble on with her grand plans for our exercise routine while we were on holiday and trusted in fate to get in her way before she managed to get me trekking up any mountains. It kept her mind off her aching head, at least.

👓 🍸 A brief digression on George

Fitness is one of many subjects on which George has strong views. He is passionate, one might almost say obsessively passionate, about animal rights. He became a committed vegetarian after we all went to see *Babe*, so that now, whenever we go out to a restaurant together, he is unbearable. As we tuck into our lamb souvlaki, George eyes us with disfavour and asks us how we can bear to eat it. Don't we remember lambs frolicking about in the sunshine, their big brown eyes gazing innocently at us, trusting, loyal, *defenceless*? How can we be so heartless? In reply Rach usually asks the waiter for extra bacon and then breaks into an impression of Babe singing 'Jingle Bells'. 'La la la-a-a! La la la-a-a! La la la-a la-la-a-a-a!' as she forks in another mouthful of meat. George says she'll be first up against the wall come the revolution.

Nor can the revolution be very far away if George has anything to do with it. He has big plans for his life once his responsibilities to Namronette Kitten Seven—Space Kitten with a Mission have ended. You'll recall he can't spend so much as a day away from home or Kitty's care might drop a fraction from his exacting standards and then he would have to commit harakiri from the shame. But at some time in the future Kitty will no longer be with us and when that day comes George plans to spend his life avenging wrongs done to animals. Apparently, there are people in deepest China who cage bears then tap their bile ducts to make aphrodisiacs. Those people are in for a big surprise when

George catches up with them. He plans to release the bears, then cage the owners and tap *their* bile ducts to make aphrodisiacs. George has bought himself a bandana, a machete and a balaclava in readiness for his life as an animal rights crusader. Luckily, Kitty is only about eight years old and living the life of Reilly so we expect her to live to at least twenty. George won't have to take his balaclava and machete to central China for a few years yet.

He doesn't believe in monogamy or commitment either, which is amusing since he's the most faithful man we know. You may be wondering why neither of us, while loving George dearly, wants to go out with him. Or you may not, depending on how sane you are. George once had a girlfriend called Mandy—a taxi driver like George, a Scrabble champ and an all round cool chick. He went out with Mandy for nine and a half years, they lived together for five of those years, spent all their time together and shared parenting duties for Namronette Kitten Seven—Space Kitten with a Mission. According to George, however, he and Mandy were not an item, not a couple and never going out—they were merely two people having a series of one-night stands. A series of one-night stands that continued unbroken for nine and a half years, as we used to point out to him. George was unmoved. Under no circumstances would he admit to commitment or fidelity. It was simply a coincidence that he had never had a one-night stand with anyone else in those nine and a half years. In the end, Mandy got jack of it and found someone who would be in a relationship with her and admit that's what he was doing. And who can blame her? Not George, to his eternal credit. They fought over

Kitty's care when they separated, but George's devotion won out and he got sole custody and guardianship.

👓 🍸 Our nation's capital

Canberra's not too hard to get into because it's at the end of the Federal Highway. Once there, however, it's a total nightmare to find your way anywhere. That's because Canberra's designers thought it would be a good idea to make all the roads circular, so there's never a direct route to follow. It's always a matter of going around in a circle one way, turning left and then going around in a circle the other way. And if you miss your turn off, you end up right back where you started. Jules thinks this road system neatly symbolises the way Australia's governed.

There is one suburb called Downer—a fabulous name. Even better, in Downer is a Terminus Street. We've always wanted to live at no. 13 Terminus Street, Downer—just to have the most depressing address in Australia.

We managed to find our way to our motel, an ordinary little grey cheapy, and dumped our stuff before heading off to get our culture hit—the reason we'd come to Canberra. We drove around and around for quite some time—took a wrong turning despite Jules' timed internet maps ('left along Coronation Circle 2 min, 20 sec') and ended up circling right back to our motel—before finally finding the (circular!) driveway of ScreenSound Australia, the national film and sound archive. There, a lovely chap showed us footage from

1896 to the present: the early Ned Kelly films, the footage of the 1896 Melbourne Cup, a 1940s Aeroplane Jelly ad. We were particularly struck by a woman who came to these shores in 1961—Sabrina. She was a Brit with big, fake blond hair, and the biggest, most strangely shaped breasts you've ever seen, pointing about three feet out in front of her at just above waist level. She featured in an ad for motor grease alongside a deeply embarrassed fellow in overalls. Every so often she remembered that she was supposed to be sexy and gave Mr Overalls a cringe-making 'moue' with her mouth while he tried hard to keep talking about grease without blushing. Very odd indeed, especially when you remember Samantha Fox. What is it with these British sex symbols? Why do we Australians turn them into starlets? What would Freud say?

From there it was on to the new National Museum, about which so much has been written. Hmmm. When you walk into the museum, the first thing you is see a whole lot of words painted on a wall—Joy, Diversity, Eternity, Harmony—and other words in the same vein. Words that give the exhibition some structure, let the visitor know what the curators think is important. These curators are caring, artistic people. Rach noted they don't pick words like Funnel Web Spider, 1975, Underarm Bowling, or even just Lamington.

The National Museum is frightfully interactive and gives you the impression that lots of very creative, caring people got together to make this museum a twenty-first century experience. Everything is multimedia enabled and desperately enthusiastic. You can just see the cardiganed creators getting excited about Vision, Interaction, Kids and Creativity. You don't just *see* this exhibition, you *hear* it and *feel* it, from the Circular Cinema that creaks around showing footage of people saying caring things about Freedom and Love to the k-Space!!! where you can put on the 3D glasses and watch a future Australia materialise before your eyes. How long did it take the Naming Committee to decide which letter of the alphabet would get the honour for that one? *It can't be e, obviously. What about j? Done to death by now, Andre . . . z? Yes, good, that has ethnic overtones. Only Central European ethnic overtones, Moya, hardly inclusive. How about q? No, I think that belongs to the gay lobby, don't you . . .*

It's all a bit much, actually, and we found ourselves longing for glass cases filled with dusty old fossils and handwritten Latin names on pieces of cardboard. And quiet. A bit more silence wouldn't hurt the National Museum. It's all so *stimulating*. You just wish it'd stop so you could just think.

Mind you, the footage of Steven Bradbury talking about his win at the Winter Olympics was great. You may remember, Steven was the guy who won our first Winter Olympics gold medal in the speed-skating race. There were five competitors in this race. Steven won when the four skaters in front of him fell over three metres before the finish line. He said he was just following his game plan and, miraculously, it worked.

'What were you thinking as you entered the home straight with four people in front of you?' asked Roy and HG.

'I was thinking "Geez my legs hurt."'

Now there's an Australian.

That was about all the culture we could stand for a day, so we went in search of a bar. Here's the thing about Canberra—it's desolate. It's nothing but wide empty streets, government buildings, museums and the occasional beanied passerby on their way to a multimedia conference. Finding nightlife is tough. We had booked into a motel 'seven minutes walk from Manuka', which is supposedly the centre of the action. Ha! Just as well Jules has a good sense of direction. We walked around in circles for a while, following lights in the distance, only to find ourselves on yet another empty suburban street. At last, though, we did come across a few cafés and restaurants in a reasonably lively bunch on a couple of street corners.

✑ And then, as if Canberra weren't bad enough already . . .

We stopped off at a bar called Verve for a refreshing mar-garita. The search for night-life had sapped the last of our energies and we slumped against the leather cubes of the lounge chairs, gazing listlessly at the cocktail menu. Suddenly, Jules gasped and shot her menu up in front of her face, 'Rach! Look over there! No, don't goggle! Subtly, for heaven's sake, or they might see us!'

I peered over my menu.

'Where? Who is it?'

'Over by the window, the couple next to the wall.'

At that moment, the cocktail waiter appeared. He was a

young, muscular, olive-skinned spunk, and he bent in close to Jules so he could look her right in the eye.

'Can I get you ladies anything?' he breathed hotly at her.

Jules was sitting stiffly, her nose almost pressed to the menu which she still had up in front of her face, 'No!' she yelped into her menu. 'Not yet, that is, we need more time.'

He looked slightly puzzled, but said smoothly, 'Of course, I'll come back in a few minutes.'

If he was looking puzzled, I was looking astounded. How could she have missed a cue like that?

'Jules, what's the matter with you?'

'It's *Tim*!' she hissed.

'Who?'

'Tim! You remember, I was going out with him when I first met you. Tim, from the Department of Fair Trading.'

'Not Tiny Tim?' I took another peek into the corner. So it was! Tiny Tim, so called because of ... well, because of his rather undersized, um, well because although size doesn't matter and indeed some of us don't actually like porn-star sized equipment there *is* a lower limit below which a man can't really go without affecting, adversely, the ... shall we say, the *penetrative* aspects of sex. And apparently Tim's penis resembled nothing so much as a fuschia Derwent pencil.

I looked at him now. He and his partner were chewing steak and talking in the unemphatic manner of two people well used to each other's conversation.

'He hasn't changed all that much, has he? Who's that with him?

'Erica!'

'Isn't that the one who came after you?'

'Yes! Oh God!'

'Um, Jules, why are you hiding?'

'I don't want him to see me. I couldn't bear it.'

'Why ever not?'

'Look at him! Here he is—a decade later—happy, fulfilled, still with the same partner; they probably have kids by now, settled, comfortable, a *family*. And here am I a decade later and I can't even get a *date*, let alone a partner or kids.'

I didn't know what to say to this. I understood her feelings but, really, Tim? She was the one who'd kicked Tim out. Was I missing the point?

The beautiful olive-skinned cocktail waiter materialised at Jules' elbow. I gave him a big, encouraging smile. Just what Jules needed to take her mind off this sudden catastrophe—a keen young man. She still had her head buried in her menu.

'Can I take your order now?' said Olive-Skin, leaning his hand on the arm of Jules' chair and smiling warmly at her.

'That'd be lovely. Jules, what are you having?'

'Eh?'

'*What are you having to drink?*'

'I can highly recommend the Slow Kiss,' said the gorgeous young waiter, and he waited for her to look up. He waited in vain.

'Jules!' I prodded her.

She started and looked at me accusingly. 'Shhhhh!'

'The waiter wants to know what you'll have to drink.'

Jules turned her rabbit-in-the-headlights gaze on the waiter, completely blind to the invitation in his eyes, and said, 'Margarita. I'll have a margarita,' as though she'd say anything to get rid of him and go back to the far more enthralling activity of hiding in her menu. He looked astonished. Whatever response he usually gets to the old come-on, I doubt it's that one. But he took our order graciously enough and went off to provide.

'Jules, have you gone completely mad? That guy was flirting outrageously with you. Even I couldn't miss the signs.'

'What? Look again, will you. Are they still there?'

'Yes.'

'How are we going to get out of here?'

'We're going to use the front door. Look, hon, why are you so upset?'

'Because *I* want family and kids,' she whispered furiously from behind her menu. '*I* want mortgage belt. *I* want companionable Saturday night dinners with nothing much to say. I threw Tim out because he didn't have everything I wanted in a man, and along came Erica and snapped him up and now *he* has all that and I'm a dateless, lonely, desperate single with no prospect of any of it. That's why I'm so upset. And I don't want him to see me like this. I feel pathetic. My life is pathetic.'

I began to understand.

'Okay, so let me ask you this. We've been one day in Canberra and already we feel like an undertaker has mistaken us for one of his customers and has started on us with the embalming fluid. We've been simultaneously deafened and bored by a multimedia frenzy and it's taken us 45 minutes to find a marginally acceptable bar. So, if you'd married Tim, you would (a) *live here*, and (b) live here with a man who . . .

well, a man whose nickname is Tiny Tim, need I say more. Don't you think you'd be just the smallest bit unhappy?'

'Hey! I'm just the smallest bit unhappy *now*. And never mind about the "tiny". There's all sorts of things you can do with surgery these days. Look at what medical science is doing to lips. The Derwent pencil is probably a raging purple love pump now, thanks to regular collagen injections.'

'I seriously doubt it.'

'I don't. I didn't get a good look at her—does she look ten years older? Do you think I should have married him?'

'She looks just like the rest of us, and no you should not have married him. You're not that unhappy, you know. I think it's just Canberra getting you down.'

'Here you go, ladies,' the gorgeous waiter put down two margaritas in front of us. 'Are you ladies in town for long?'

Jules ignored the question, dropped her menu and covered her face with the margarita glass instead. In three seconds, she'd drained it. 'Come on, Rach, we have to go,' she said, throwing money on the table and grabbing my hand.

'But I haven't finished.'

'You walk on that side,' she edged me between her and Tim.

'Have a good evening, ladies,' said the bemused young waiter, and we stumbled past him to the exit, Jules pulling on my elbow and keeping her head down.

Once outside Jules said to me, 'No-one even flirts with me any more.' I didn't have the heart to tell her that she could have broken her drought that very night. Who wants to break a drought in Canberra, anyway? I walked her back to the motel, listening to my old friend having a momentary break from sanity. All she could talk about was Tim and Erica and their supposedly perfect family life compared to her single, and therefore failed, life. I tried to point out that we had no idea whether or not Tim and Erica were happy but Jules was having none of it. I reminded her that Tim, although a nice man, had been just dull enough to make the prospect of a lifetime with him unthinkable, and that was why she had put an end to their relationship, quite apart from the physical drawback. I might as well have kept my mouth shut. Jules didn't want to be logical; she wanted to grieve.

When we got back to our hotel, I put on the kettle, raided the minibar and made her a hot toddy in the hope that alcohol would bring her back to her senses. I ran her a bath and opened the second miniature brandy and the Toblerone. From the bathroom, Jules carried on some more about her many failures and likely future failures—no husband, no kids, no grandchildren, lonely forgotten old age, undistinguished career, expanding waistline, no sex for the rest of her life, miserable weekends, financially disadvantaged, pointless existence. She went on and on. Seeing Tim had really thrown a switch. I waited for her to talk it out and then, just as I was thinking I'd better kill her for the good of mankind and my own sanity, the brandy and the bubbles started to take effect and she began to recall Tim as he actually was, not as she felt he must surely have been—a nice enough man who carefully had no opinion on anything at all, who thought men were logical and women emotional, and who became socially paralysed when confronted with anyone not white and upper middle class.

'Add to this, Rach, add to this, the fact that he has actually chosen to live in Canberra and seems to be happy here.'

This was more like it. Couldn't be much longer now and she'd have talked herself down from her existential ledge. When she'd finished in the bath I supplied her with a second hot toddy and the chocolate and we settled into our beds. Jules' panic had subsided and she was beginning to think that the very fact she could choose to leave Canberra any time she liked and never return was good enough reason to be grateful she'd never married Tim. Seizing my moment, I proposed we indulge in one of life's great luxuries—telly in bed. That sealed her recovery. We finished the Toblerone while watching two episodes of 'NYPD Blue' back to back and by lights out Jules had ceased thinking about Tim and was telling me all about Angelo, a man at her gym who closely resembles the Latino guy in 'NYPD Blue'. Normal service had been resumed.

⌣ 𝖸 We leave the nation's capital to its own devices

Breakfast next morning revealed one of the trials of motel life—the bus tour. The dining room was filled with about 40 000 Italian pensioners on a tour of Australia. We stood in a long, long queue for toast, which the slowly revolving toaster was slowly dispensing. Then we squeezed ourselves onto a corner of a table and tried to drink our filter coffee while tiny Italian women bustled around at waist height, jabbering excitedly to each other. Their husbands looked almost as morose and resentful as we were. We muttered to each other about the treachery of motel owners who don't alert guests to the imminent invasion of the dining room.

Staggering away, our ears ringing, we decided that what we needed was a nice, quiet, contemplative sort of tourist attraction, so we headed out in the early morning sunshine for Floriade, Canberra's annual flower extravaganza. Floriade has a different theme each year, because after all who would come just to see the beautiful flowers? And more importantly, what would be the point of having a marketing department if they didn't add value? This year the primary flower was tulips and the theme, for some reason, space travel. What that meant was swathes and swathes of tulips interspersed with circles of pansies, designed to create the impression that an alien spacecraft had landed there. Again with the circles—it's in Canberra's blood. And here again, the multi-media mafia had been roped in. Just as we were gazing in soul-swelling silence at a particularly glorious tulip and pansy display we were rocked off our socks by the sudden irruption of a hammy actor bellowing, 'I am Zorg from the planet Ergatron' from behind a tree. It was a sound system, volume up full blast, desperately trying to give us the multi-dimensional 'space' experience. Sigh.

We quickly walked away in search of a little peace and quiet so we could really appreciate what the gardeners had created. And they had created magic. We spent an hour strolling through the gardens taking it all in. Just as we came to the end of our walk we spied five tour buses disgorging our 40 000 Italian pensioners. God knows what they made of the multi-media paradise that is Canberra, and we weren't staying to find out. We made our exit through the Scarecrow Walk where local businesses and cultural groups had created their own representative scarecrows. We kinda wished the local pharmacist had gone to a bit more effort—his was just a lot of bandage boxes stuck together; whereas some enterprising high school kids had made one that strongly resembled the mighty-breasted Sabrina.

Jules makes us visit Goulburn to satisfy a ridiculous obsession

Not that Goulburn isn't a lovely place—it just wasn't on our itinerary, and it's at least an hour away from Canberra, or more if you're with Jules who wants to stop at every boutique winery on the way, and believe me there are lots of boutique wineries between Canberra and Goulburn.

We headed for Goulburn for one reason and one reason only—Jules is desperate to see the Big Merino. According to her, a trip just isn't a trip until you've seen something BIG. From Canberra, it is only an hour to the Big Merino so she forced us to make a 'small detour'.

'We'd have got here faster if you didn't try to stop at every vineyard we passed.'

'Wine is an Australian staple and our fastest growing export,' replied Jules. We have a patriotic duty to keep abreast of developments.'

Whatever. I'd always pictured the Big Merino out in a paddock, standing majestically on its own. I'd have driven right past the actual Big Merino except that Jules burst into spontaneous applause and gleeful shouts when she saw it. It's in a petrol station.

'It's gorgeous!'

'It's a gift shop with a sheep spray-concreted onto its roof and walls.'

'It's Australian. Ooh, look Rach, it says it's the World's Biggest Merino. Not Australia's biggest merino—the *World's* biggest merino.'

'I wonder where the World's Second Biggest Merino is. The Buzz Aldrin of sheep statuary.'

'Ooh! Mini versions in real sheepskin. I have to have this for my collection.'

Yes, Jules has a collection of mini Big Icons. She's got the mini Big Oyster, the mini Big Prawn, the mini Big Banana and the mini Big Pineapple—she has that one in a snowdome. But you know, Jules is on to something. At least the Big Merino is just that. A big sheep in a big country that likes to build big things. And the closest it comes to multimedia is the gold spotlights they turn on every night to give it that majestic look.

CHAPTER SIX

Excitement at last

 We go north, not south

Back in the car, I was hoping Jules would be too preoccupied with her snowdomes to notice that I was heading us north to Bathurst rather than south to the ski fields. Sometimes there's no point trying to get people to see reason—you just have to take a firm hand and direct fate for yourself. Jules had forgotten all about the horror of her bike ride. Her butt had that virtuous 'I've been worked hard and I feel fractionally tauter than I did before' feeling and she was all fired up about our holiday exercise regimen. She was firmly of the view that we should now head to the Snowy Mountains and go on an extended hike—rising at dawn, bathing in the icy morning river and trekking over the range. The sight of a pair of straining bike riders on the highway made her pause briefly, but she soon shook off this moment of weakness.

I had protested that I didn't want to go hiking, but Jules said it was 'good for us' and having skilfully occupied the moral high ground there was no point my trying to argue her down from it. So, being the driver, I simply turned left instead of right at the highway while Jules was inspecting her miniature merino, and kept her chatting about the culture of the Big Icon, figuring that if I got us far enough along the road to Bathurst, she'd accept her fate.

I'd had a quick look at the map and decided to head to Oberon via Taralga on a road that went through the Abercrombie River National Park. Although I'm not much of a one for hiking through it, I'm a very big fan of the bush, and I'd spotted a country road on the map that would take us to Oberon. I was determined that we should take it. If Jules has a fault, it's her need to stay on six-lane highways just because they've been built. Left to myself, I'd have taken the Old Federal Highway to Canberra, not the whizz bang new motorway. The old highway is a one-lane-south-one-lane-north, winding death trap and I love it. It's overhung by gum trees, the bushland snuggles up against it and farms are so close cows look you straight in the eye as you roar past at 70 clicks, the maximum speed anyone past their teenage years is willing to go. The motorway is a twelve-lane dead straight horror bounded by concrete sound barriers. Sure, the road toll is down, and, yes, you can get to Canberra in three hours instead of six—but where's the romance? Where's the sense of freedom? And, more importantly, where's the bush? It's hidden behind an ugly concrete slab. You can't even smell it because if you wind your window down your head gets blown off by truck backdraft and exhaust. It's not that I'm against progress (although I don't own a computer or a video player, my TV is 25 years old with no remote control, and I'm not absolutely certain what a DVD is), it's just that I prefer older, slower things. Like Jules. Sorry about that—couldn't resist.

So I headed north up the Hume Highway, surreptitiously keeping an eye out for the country road turn off to Taralga. With any luck, Jules would be too happy playing with her new toys to notice this slight ignoring of her wishes. We hadn't been going very long when I spotted a sign for a vineyard Jules had wanted to visit just before we got to the Big Merino. Good Lord, I thought, the place must be absolutely enormous—it starts before Goulburn and ends after it. Agricultural real estate is like that in Australia. You don't call it a farm unless you can fit Belgium on it with room to spare for the dog. I was sure it was the same vineyard because of its name—Kuntbungle Cellars. Yes, Kuntbungle. What's happened to censorship in this country, that's what I want to know. We used to be a proud nation of wet blankets—we don't care if you call it art, you can take it back to bloody Greece where it belongs. There'll be no sex here, thanks very much. So I'm mighty proud of the humorous folk at Kuntbungle Cellars, unless of course they're German and that's actually their name . . . naaah.

The turn off to Taralga was further away than it had seemed on the map. Jules was happily absorbed in her mini sheep when I saw an ACT information centre. I was just about to give her a nudge and share the joke—what on earth did the ACT think it was doing putting an information centre in NSW? Idiots. You only visit the information centre when you get to the place you need the information on. No wonder the tourism industry is plummeting in Canberra. Luckily, I remembered just in time that Jules thought we *were* in the ACT, but it was a close call. I'd got as far as saying, 'Hey Jules . . .' before I remembered, and had to say, '. . . ummm . . . we should send a postcard to George.' Lame, I know, but I was under pressure. I quickly occupied her attention by inviting her to compose a card to George telling him all about the Big Merino. That kept her mind off the road for another fifteen minutes. But in all that time, the Taralga road never came into view.

I was getting a bit annoyed with this turn off not appearing. Where in the Sam Hill was it? My eyes positively ached from trying to read the green signs that tell you how far to the next town. I was surprised to see Canberra on one of these signs, but I assumed that there must be a turn off to Canberra coming up. I was concentrating so hard that I'd stopped talking altogether.

Jules looked up from her real wool mini merino and broke the silence. 'You'll have to turn onto the Monaro soon.'

'What?'

'You'll have to turn left onto the Monaro Highway soon or we'll end up in Canberra again. Look out for the sign to Cooma.'

'Cooma? We're not going to Cooma, we're going to Bathurst!'

'Then why are we heading south?'

'We're not heading south, we're heading north.'

'Uh huh. So why does that sign say "Canberra 50 km"?'

'It's another route . . . isn't it?'

'We're on the Federal Highway going south to Canberra. If you wanted to go north to Bathurst you'd need to follow the road to Oberon.'

Long pause.

'Rach, were you trying to sneak us into Bathurst without my noticing?' She was valiantly trying not to laugh. My frustration burst out.

'Oh, for God's sake, Jules! I don't want to go trekking in the Snowy Mountains. I'm sure it'll be frightfully good for my butt, but I. Don't. Care. I want to have a nice peaceful camp in a National Park next to a river. I want to read by the campfire at night and commune with the wallabies in the morning. I do NOT want to challenge my body to be the best it can be. Ever.'

'That's okay. If you really don't want to go to the Snowy, then we don't have to. I don't mind going to Bathurst, but you'd better turn around.'

'You won't regret that decision!' and I chucked a U-ey at the next right.

After a while, travelling north this time, Jules said, 'Didn't you notice the sign for Kuntbungle Cellars?'

'Yes . . . I just thought it must be very big. Yes, all right you can stop laughing any time you like.' But she didn't, and who can blame her.

'You know, Rach, you've been doing all the driving. Why don't I take over and you can navigate.'

'Is that irony?'

'No, really. I mean it.'

'I want to take this road here—see? The one that goes via Taralga.'

'Uh huh. Keep your eyes on the road.'

☙ Jules gets behind the wheel and reflects on the life of a little known poet

So we headed north with me at the wheel—real north, not Rach north. It's a funny thing about Rach, no matter how many times she goes the wrong way she's absolutely convinced she can navigate. When we were travelling around Europe with a bunch of friends, if we got lost and didn't know which way to go, we'd say, 'Hey Rach, which way would you go?' Rach would give it her serious consideration and say, 'Left. I'd go left,' and that was enough for the gang— 'Okay everyone, right it is.' And she'd twist her mouth up and say one day we'd be sorry, but that day never came and every time she turned out to be wrong she'd look astonished and say, 'Well, I'll be! I could have sworn it was left!' Right now she's looking at the map, then up at the road, then down at the map, and counting the roads we pass until the turn off to Oberon. Lucky thing I looked at the map myself— we might actually get there.

You know, we've talked about what I do for a living, but I don't think anyone's mentioned Rach's career. She's a poet. Yes, a poet. Not a successful poet, not even a published poet, although she has won prizes, or to be more specific, a prize—the West Wyalong Regional Librarians' Literary Award

(Category: Urban Poetry—Unpublished). Prize—$50 and a certificate. She's never once been paid to write verse but that's her career and she gets very upset if you call her a technical assistant, even though that's what she actually does for a living, and has done ever since she accidentally graduated from her English degree in 1994. It had taken her nine years to get through a four-year undergraduate course and she was rather hoping to stretch it out for another couple of years before having to find a real job. Unfortunately, in 1994, the year she began what was supposed to be the first of many years getting through the honours curriculum, she got interested in Chaucer and wrote a decent paper. Before she'd managed to rectify her mistake, she was standing on a podium shaking the Vice-Chancellor's right hand as he firmly passed her her degree with his left.

The university kept her on—out of pity I suppose—giving her a job setting up rooms for lectures. Someone thought she'd be good with technical stuff—some idiot they've since fired, I should hope. I don't think they've had a crisis-free day since 1995. It took years to train her on the equipment. Then, just when she'd got the whole floppy disk/PowerPoint thing under her belt, some smart alec in Japan invented the DVD and the university decided it had better be at the forefront of technology. Poor Rach! She took to convincing lecturers that the equipment was broken and wouldn't they rather use their PowerPoint prez from last year? Since the lecturers were as puzzled by the new equipment as she was, everyone agreed that, perhaps, last year's presentation having gone down so well with the students, yes, perhaps that would be safer than risking the disappointment of no pictures at all. It's amazing how many people she managed to convince. If one of the more up-to-date lecturers got stubborn and insisted on the DVD, she just took all the leads and 'lost' them in the cleaner's anteroom, so they'd end up having to use the old overhead projector. That sorted them out.

Her crowning achievement was the day she blew the entire university's electricity system by overloading the fuses in the main theatre. She'd set up the theatre for a lecture by the famous international literary critic Harold Bloom, who'd come all the way from America to enlighten the students on the meaning of the Kaballah. It was quite a coup for the faculty—not the power failure, Harold Bloom. They'd advertised it for months: the Head of School was counting on the kudos to get her a professorship in the next round of appointments; the Dean was taking all the credit.

When the day came, the students packed out the biggest theatre on campus and every dignitary and their dog claimed reserved seats at the front. The great man stood on the podium, looking like Caesar contemplating the Ancient Britons before Boadicea stuck her oar in. The students thundered their applause. He approached the microphone, the applause died down. Bloom looked down at his hands and cleared his throat, the audience held its collective breath. The head technician watched the master intently, his finger poised over the microphone switch, waiting for his moment. Beside him, in the role of able assistant, stood Rach, staring into space trying to think of a rhyme for 'multilateral'. Bloom stepped up to the lectern—the moment had arrived. The head technician flicked the *Mic On* switch, there was a blinding flash of light, a puff of smoke, a terrific explosion—then darkness. And silence. A voice was heard in the gloom, 'Hello? What happened to the lights?' Then some choking sounds from the technical booth as the head technician tried to put an early end to a budding poet's life. Pandemonium erupted in the hall, through which the sounds of an annoyed literary critic's footsteps could faintly be heard heading to the airport.

Excitement comes our way

It's not that Rach is not bright, because she is; it's just that the real world has to fight for space in her head while she daydreams in rhyming couplets. You think the map thing is bad, but it's not just maps; it's forms and tax returns and electricity bills. They all pass her by in a blur of incomprehension. Luckily, the university only has to clean up after her three days a week. The rest of the time she works as a temp, misfiling important documents for various public service agencies.

So I don't lightly let her loose on navigational duty but she had done most of the driving, so it seemed only fair. To my surprise we found the road easily enough and swung off the highway onto the smaller road. Rach is right about secondary roads—they are much more pleasant to drive on. She wanted to have a picnic lunch on the Bolong River, because she is crazy about rivers, so I let her navigate us on what seemed like a pretty straightforward route to the river. There were a few roads to choose from and we were careful to pick the one that looked the most navigable. I could have sworn we'd chosen a tar road but ten minutes in the tar turned to gravel, then clay, and then the worst surface of all.

'Oh crap,' I said. 'It's sand,' and I slowed to 40. The car slid a little but stayed fairly stable.

'Maybe we should turn back.' Rach had stopped composing odes to the countryside and was lightly gripping the dashboard.

'No, she'll be right as long as I drive carefully,' and as I said those words the back of the car started to fishtail out of control.

I could hear Rach's, 'Uh oh,' and my mind froze. Everything slowed down and I couldn't remember—what do you do when you're in a fishtail? Then I heard George's voice, 'Don't brake. Whatever you do, don't brake! Turn the wheel hard into the direction of the slide. Turn the wheel hard into the direction of the slide!' The trouble with turning the wheel into the slide is, it goes against every instinct. I wanted to brake. I desperately wanted to stop. My foot hovered over the brake, my hand grasped the gear stick. I looked over at Rach. My God, what if I kill her? Then Rach put her hand on my arm, bless her, and said in a completely calm voice, 'It'll be okay, Jules. We'll be okay.'

'Stop looking at Rach and TURN HARD INTO THE SLIDE!' shouted George's image. I geared down to third, waited for the next slide and ripped the steering wheel hard right. The car swung around, the countryside slid past us and we skidded, skidded, skidded for what seemed my entire life until we gently hit the bank. The car stopped. We were still alive. We sat in silence for a minute just looking at each other, and then we couldn't stop smiling. Everyone was still alive. Thank you George Taxi—man of the moment.

The car was still running, so I switched it off and we

got out to inspect the damage. But first, a hug. We hung onto each other and laughed and laughed. Okay, now for the car. The damage wasn't too bad. One of the hubs was pressed up against the wheel, so we got out the jack and levered it off as much as we could. It was still pressing against the wheel but the car could go.

I had a look at the map. 'According to my calculations, this road will take us to Black Springs.'

So we got back in the car and slowly, oh so slowly, we hobbled our way into Black Springs, a one-horse town with a pub, a general store and—yippee-yi-ay!—a mechanic. And what a mechanic! Ah, country men, you can't beat 'em. This one was all shoulders and slow, sweet smile. I took one look at him and suddenly felt all Southern. 'We had an accident. Can you get our car back in driving condition for us?' I was trying to sound normal, but somehow my voice went all soft and helpless and my eyelids batted, apparently of their own accord. I heard Rach give a muffled snort in the background. I ignored her.

Well, of course he could fix our car. All he had to do was lift the hubcap off the wheel, but the man in him responded to 'helpless little ol' me' and he said maybe he'd better check out the rest of the car, make sure we'd be okay. Were we heading to Oberon?

'Uh huuuuuh.' There was no mistaking the hint of Southern belle in my voice.

'Come far?' He hoisted up the bonnet, and the muscles in his arms rippled.

'Uh huuuuh.' I'd lost the power of speech.

'What's taking you to Oberon?'

'We're on our way to a gay and lesbian hostel,' said Rach, heartily. The mechanic hit his head on the bonnet. She could hardly keep the laughter out of her voice as she threw this spanner into my works. I glowered at her but she was unrepentant. Rach thinks there are times when you have to put a good joke before a friendship. She'll keep.

The mechanic finished his inspection and sent us on our way. 'That's all right ladies, no charge necessary for a little thing like that. You take care on the roads, now.'

I gave him a last long look out of habit and we left the one-horse town and its divine mechanic forever. We decided to skip the picnic by the river and head straight to civilisation and the tar roads of Bathurst, my old university town.

🍸 Where Jules learned her pick-up techniques

You might be wondering about my smooth style when it comes to picking up men. I was a late developer when I was a kid, and I owe everything I know about sex, men, drinking and partying to the friendship of one woman— Lisa Kilkenny, the queen of cool. Lisa arrived at our school when she was fourteen and I had never seen anything like her outside of the movies. She had a 21-year-old boyfriend at a time when I had barely registered the implications of two sexes. Lisa wore sheer stockings and makeup when the rest of us were decked out in cottontail undies and hockey sticks. Her mum was young and bosomy and her dad leered at all her teenage friends. Lisa smoked with her cig held between her third and fourth finger, rather than second and third. Actually I never thought she quite pulled that one off, but you had to give her mega points for trend setting.

For some reason, Lisa chose to be friends with daggy, freckled, curly red-headed me, and my education began. I learned how to put on makeup, walk in high heels and do up the zip on skin-tight jeans using a coat-hanger. I trailed behind her to pubs and watched open-mouthed as she picked up boys. I learned the meaning of the words 'condom', 'roach' and 'stomach pump'. From Lisa I learned the art of pretending to be much dumber than I really was, and completely helpless, in order to attract men. I was partly appalled and partly exhilarated by just how easy this was to do. Luckily, Lisa also taught me never to believe your own bullshit so I did well in my HSC, as did she, and we went to Charles Sturt University, Bathurst, together.

At Charles Sturt, Lisa and I really came into our own. By now we were equals. No longer woman-of-the-world and her acolyte, we were partners in the crime of living life to the full. It must have been the combination of country air, country men and living away from disapproving parental gaze (you can imagine what my parents thought of Lisa's influence on my development), but Lisa and I went crazy. We knew every pub and party place in town—and they knew us. We sashayed around town playing expert pool, drinking Harvey Wallbangers and driving pick-up trucks in the middle of the night, blind drunk, around the Mount Panorama circuit. It's a miracle I'm alive to tell the tale.

It was at this time that Lisa perfected the art of the helpless pick-up. Her last boyfriend at school had been a mechanic so she knew a fair bit about cars, but she also knew the shortest way to a man's heart. One night we were driving up the main street of Bathurst when Lisa spotted a bloke she thought she'd seen the night before, a bloke she thought she'd like to get to know better. He was walking to the pub with a group of his mates. In an instant, she had pulled over to the side of the road, popped the hood and was standing gazing at the engine as if to say, 'I'm fairly sure this thing runs the—what did you call it—"car"? But now I don't know what to do.'

Her timing was perfect.

'Are you all right there?' The boys, being gentlemen, stopped to help a lady in distress.

'Oh,' said Lisa looking doe-eyed and helpless, 'there's something wrong with my car.'

'Well, let's see what the matter is,' and they all clustered around the front of the car looking knowledgeable.

'Looks like it's the carby,' said one of the boys. Somehow it's always the 'carby'.

'The what?' cooed Lisa, who knew very well what a carby was and that it had nothing whatever to do with the carby.

'Can you start her up?'

I did the honours.

'Oh!' cried Lisa. 'You've fixed it!' as the engine caught.

'Didn't really do much,' said the object of Lisa's desire.

'Oh, thank you. We were sooooo worried,' Lisa wasn't going to let modesty undo all her good work. Twenty minutes later she was in the pub gazing adoringly into the eyes of her rescuer.

Bathurst was where I picked up my taste for real men. Men who wear overalls and know how to change washers. Men who have big hands and hard bodies. Men who . . .

✎ Rach tells the story of Marlene and the action men

'Oh, will you put a sock in it! Enough already with the real men talk. You and Lisa are the only girls I know who've had a lifetime of great sex. It's outrageous. And unfair.'

'I haven't had sex in two years!'

'Except with the French Farce.'

'Like I said, I haven't had sex in two years.'

'You're right. Bad sex doesn't count. But at least you've had men flocking around you, wanting to be with you. Have you tried picking up a man lately? I don't know what's happened to them, but they've gone really, really strange. What about Marlene and the action men?'

'Okay, yes, the story of Marlene and the action men is weird.'

Our friend Marlene is possibly the sexiest girl on the face of this earth, Lisa and Marilyn Monroe excepted of course. She's always been like a candle to male moths, and she married early. Eight years into the marriage her husband left her for her best friend. Now *there's* a class act. But Marlene's a robust girl, so she figured she'd just get out on the town, start dating and marry again. She was surprised to find that somehow, without her noticing, the dating scene has changed. Men have gone strange. And real men are no longer the reliable lovers and partners they once were.

Unlike the rest of us, Marlene still recalls how to date and she still attracts men—but not just any old men either. Marlene manages to find action men. Get this, if you will. Marlene has been out, in succession, with a stuntman, a fireman, a cowboy and, wait for it, a *jet fighter pilot*. I didn't think there was such a thing as a jet fighter pilot outside Tom Cruise, but there is, and Marlene's dated him. He was a Brit and he'd fought in the Falklands, Kosovo and Iraq. Cool, huh? But here's the spooky thing. Each one of them dated her for about a fortnight, everything seemed to be going okay, then just as quickly as they came (and we speak of the stuntman, here), they left. Just stopped calling. Disappeared off the horizon. What is that about? How can you date four action men in a row and have each of them simply drop you like a stone? Maybe it's something to do with being an action man. 'Ah'm a wanderin' soul, Ma'am. Ah got a woman in every port.' The mystery of Marlene and the disappearing action men remains unsolved to this day.

It's not just Marlene—it's an epidemic. Sometimes I think my life is like a scene from *Bedazzled*. If I like them, they're sure to be gay, or married, or uninterested in me, or emotional basket cases, or *female*. I feel like saying to God, Okay, when I asked you to send me love, I meant the kind that I'll be able to enjoy. It is pointless sending me the love of my life in, say, the body of woman. Or to send along fascinating men I could talk to forever who are not interested in me. Or to make my live-in companion of twelve years a dumb animal. Yes, Thelma loves me and wants to spend every minute of her day cuddled up on my lap or gazing adoringly into my eyes. That's very lovely; however, Thelma is a cat. I remember someone said to Germaine Greer, 'Your dogs must be good company.' And she gave the poor sap a freezing look and said, 'They're dogs. Of course they're not good company. If I want company I invite people over.' Exactly. Bravo, Germs.

Bathurst

When we finally made it to Bathurst, the sun was nearly down. We put up at a pub for the night, so we could just hang out there and then stagger up to bed. Jules sharked a couple of guys at pool out of sheer nostalgia, but none of them took our fancy. Jules said flannelette shirts didn't look as appealing as they had in her uni days, and none of them looked sufficiently emotionally scarred, cold or female to suit my tastes, so we drank moderately, chatted to a few friendly locals, played a bit of pool (until they wised up to J) and went to bed early to dream of pick-up trucks. At least, *I* dreamed of pick-up trucks and I assume that Freud would have something clever to say about that.

CHAPTER SEVEN

Horsey girls and bad, bad men

👓 🍸 **We head to the Blue Mountains and chronicle Rach's tragic boyfriend choices**

The next day we set off early on the Great Western Highway, heading towards Katoomba. We briefly contemplated taking a secondary road, but after our near-death experience neither of us was feeling particularly brave, so we pottered out onto the main road and joined the reticulated lorries in the slow lane, leaving the Saabs to overtake us at 4000 miles per hour.

'Notice how this highway is crawling with luxury cars?' said Rach. 'You know why that is, don't you?'

'No, why?'

'It's the Blue Mountains. We're on the outskirts of the Orthodontist Zone.'

'What's the Orthodontist Zone?' asked Jules, obediently.

'Ah! I'm glad you asked. The Orthodontist Zone is the lower reaches of the Blue Mountains—it's countryside, yet only an hour and a half from Macquarie Street by express train. This is where all the tax lawyers, plastic surgeons and orthodontists came to live after the plumbers moved into Rose Bay. They weighed up ageing, dope-smoking hippies over vigorous, upwardly mobile plumbers and the hippies seemed less of a threat to their world order. So they moved to the Blue Mountains to foul up a perfectly lovely bit of Australian bush with their four-wheel drives and Saab convertibles.'

'I love the Blue Mountains.'

'Jules, you love everything. You love life. You're a throwback. No-one's enthusiastic about life anymore. While we're all rolling in Western wealth and cynicism, you're as full of *joie de vivre* as Heidi. You have to be more like Heidi's bitter old grandfather if you don't want to stand out from the Sydney crowd.'

'More like you, you mean.'

'Am I bitter?' said Rach.

'Not really bitter, no, but you do spend a lot of your life cooped up in your living room, just like Heidi's grandfather.'

'That's why it's called a living room. You live in it. Otherwise it would be called the just-passing-on-my-way-out room.'

'Some of us manage to live in pubs, or restaurants, or theatres, or any place where other people gather to socialise.'

'To what?'

'To *socialise*. Meet people. See new and different things.'

'But I don't like meeting people,' said Rach. 'I like being by myself.'

'How are you going to find a lover if you don't get out of your house?'

There was a long pause while Rach thought that one over.

'I rest my case,' said Jules.

'No wait, I'm still thinking.'

'I have you over a barrel, my friend.'

'No you don't! I've remembered now. I'm looking for a man who'll leave me alone, not bother me too much.'

'You're succeeding there,' said Jules. 'All the men you fall in love with leave you well alone.'

A slightly worried pause followed. 'Is that what's happening? Am I going for men who won't come anywhere near me?' Rach was feeling uneasy.

Jules chose her words carefully. The time had come to whip out the couch and give a close friend insight. 'How long were you with Byron?'

'Four years.'

'And in four years, was he ever sober?'

'Not to my knowledge.'

'No. Was he faithful?'

'No,' said Rach.

'In four years, did you ever live together?'

'Once, for about six weeks.'

'And?'

'It was so awful I chucked him out and ended the relationship.'

'So, in all that time, you never lived together, he was always somewhere between slightly sozzled and smashed, and he was sleeping around.'

'Yes, but he was very funny and very charming. And he wasn't absolutely legless the whole time.'

'He was legless on every social occasion I can recall.' Jules pressed the point.

'But still very funny. And clever—I liked talking to him.'

'Now that's something all your partners, since I've known you anyway, have in common. They're smart and they're thinkers and they're charming, but they're totally unavailable in every other sense. What about Ricardo?'

Ah, Ricardo

Ah, Ricardo. Jules was referring to my lover before Byron. And now that she's mentioned it, I can see a spooky resemblance between Ricardo and Byron. Ricardo and I went out for two and a half years. He was another charming, amusing layabout. He'd managed to get himself a cushy job in the public service which required so little effort that he was able to indulge in his twin passions, gambling and drinking, from lunch time to heads down at night. He, too, was rarely sober, but he was a happy drunk, and a bit of spunk to boot. He had a pair of leather pants which I recall with some delight to this day. And, like Byron, we were okay while I was still freely living on my own. It was getting closer that spelled the end.

Charming though he was, Ricardo was not a man you could talk to about your most intimate feelings. He lived on a permanent level of Hail-Fellow-Well-Met-ness, never owning up to any feelings other than happiness and/or pleasure. He certainly seemed permanently okay, but he could behave very oddly at times. I could never put my finger on what it was that made, say, his obsessive need to cook a three-course meal in the middle of the night, so disturbing. And since he himself could never explain his odder moments, other than to say, 'It makes me happy', I stopped worrying about what it meant and simply accepted the midnight cooking, the permanent cheeriness, and all that went with it.

After two and a half years we decided it was time to live together, so Ricardo, Thelma and I moved into a terrace house in Newtown. Three weeks later, he spent our entire life savings in four and a half hours on a Saturday afternoon at the race track. That was enough for me—Thelma and I moved out and severed relations with the lovely, yet fatal, Ricardo. It was in the move that I made a crucial discovery. I had taken my camping gear out of the back of a cupboard and was emptying out the eskies for a stocktake. I opened my smallest esky and found inside a gross of needles. It appeared Ricardo had a third passion of which I was unaware, but which did explain some of his more peculiar behaviour.

There's a coda to this story. A few months after we split, Ricardo did a typically Ricardo thing. It was the middle of winter, pouring with rain, at the end of the working day. I came out of my office building and there, standing on the pavement under a giant red umbrella, was Ricardo. He simply walked up to me and put the umbrella over both of us. Without saying a word, he caught the bus home with me, came up to my flat and, when we got inside, turned on the TV and flung himself on the floor, exactly as though we were still living together. All this without a word. And I went along with it. He had that kind of personality. Without knowing how, you always ended up doing what Ricardo wanted. There he was, lying on the floor of my new home, watching TV as though nothing had happened. Thelma stalked around him looking miffed, but then Thelma had never been a big fan of Ricardo's. When bedtime came, Ricardo came with me. Apparently he had moved back in.

Now, my house is not a miracle of cleanliness. I tend to leave stuff lying around, and on this occasion I'd let the washing go to such an extent that I was down to the flares and boob tubes (long before they came back in fashion). When Ricardo discarded his clothes on the floor, they melted into the sea of my own clothes. Next morning, we woke up to a familiar smell for anyone who's lived with Thelma—cat wee. Thelma had gone to the trouble of searching out Ricardo's clothing on the floor and giving his shorts a good soaking. That she managed to miss all my clothes is a testament to her aim and skill. Her message was unmistakable. I gave Ricardo a pair of my shorts as a farewell gift and told him never to come back again. My own instincts might be shot but Thelma's are spot on, and I trust her judgement absolutely.

Maybe Jules had a point. There was something else that my relationships with Ricardo and Byron had in common, but I wasn't ready to tell Jules yet. Maybe later. When we're drunk. And I can make sensitive admissions about sex.

♟ Jules continues her grilling

'What did George have to say about the detective?'

'He said, "Are you mad? Don't you know that all men are bastards and detectives are super bastards?" He was quite eloquent on the subject. He said what the hell did I think I was doing even looking at a man whose job requires him to play power games with vicious criminals, keeping all emotional reactions locked away. Did I really think a man like that was going to suit an overly sensitive flower like me?'

'And what did you say?'

'I said, "I am not overly sensitive. The world is a brutal place and only some of us can see it."'

'No, about the detective . . . '

'Oh. I said I liked talking to him. He was a really interesting guy. I don't find all that many people fascinating, but this one was.'

'And what did George say?'

'He said, "Well, you like talking to me but you've got enough sense not to fall in love with me. Couldn't you try to be just as discriminating with other men?"'

'He has a point,' said Jules. 'I mean, really Rach, a detective. You have to be kidding. You're a poet, for chrissakes. You do tend to fall in love with ludicrously unsuitable men.'

'And women.'

'And women. See? Are you gay?'

'Mmmmm. No.'

'No. And if you were you'd only fall in love with women

who couldn't come out of the closet. Don't look at me like that—you know that's true. You make lifetime partner choices that give your loving friends grey hairs.'

'You see why I stay at home, then. I'm keeping out of harm's way.'

'I don't think giving up altogether is the answer,' said Jules. 'You just need to get into life a bit more. Get out of the house. Meet people.'

'I go to the university three times a week. Does that count as getting out of the house?'

'Sure, it's a start. Is there anyone there you like?'

'Yeah, there's one I thought I might like to get to know.'

'And?'

'I got to know him.'

'And?'

'He asked me for George's phone number.'

'Ah.'

'He was surprised to find that George wasn't gay.'

'We must tell George.'

'Do people who are into life like the Blue Mountains?' Rach didn't think that anything was going to get her to like the Blue Mountains.

'What's your beef with the Blue Mountains?'

✍ Rach and the word 'twee'

What's my beef? You take a perfectly lovely environment like the Blue Mountains, all eucalyptus and craggy rock, then fill it with plastic surgeons, Saabs and superannuated hippies making a mockery of all that the hippy credo stood for by running Ye Olde Curiosity Gifte Shoppe featuring Granma's Home-made Lime and Emu Beak Marmalade and Mrs McGinty's Lavender Bath Oil, Soap and Foot Creme Gifte Packe. It's obscene! It's a travesty! It's a national disgrace! It's TWEE!

I can recall one of the professors at our university on exchange from Germany asking me whether or not he should visit the Three Sisters. I told him the Three Sisters are terrific, not to be missed, don't leave Australia without paying them a visit. Just be sure to go straight there and straight back. Look neither to the right nor the left, I told him. Don't be tempted to stop off at Ye Olde Katoomba Village for a quick jam scone and a coffee. Have a gander at the Three Sisters, then get the hell out of there, I said to him, or you'll drown in a thick soup of twee. He asked me what is the meaning of 'twee', please. And do you know, I couldn't think of a good definition. I knew what it was all right—it was pots of jam with checked cloth caps and scented rosehip candle gift packs—but how to put that into a couple of words? It took me two days before I finally came up with the answer— twee means self-consciously cute. And that's why I hate the Blue Mountains. It's self-consciously cute. It should be put out to pasture along with its ageing hippy residents.

As I've been telling you this, Jules has stopped for a bite to eat and you should only see the place she's chosen. It's in one of those awful, folksy 'villages' that infest the Blue Mountains in their thousands. Jules claims that this place makes bread to die for. It had better, because someone's going to die if I don't get out of here soon. This café of which she speaks so highly is a ghastly little faux Austrian restaurant, desperately trying to convince itself and the voting public that it's the real McCoy. Ha! I've been to Austria and restaurants in that noble land do not cover their windows with two rows of fake lace curtains. They do not put ruffles on their chairs or doilies under pink candles. And when they give you blackforest cake, they give you a seriously large piece of chocolate and cherry heaven with no stinting on the whipped cream.

'No really, Jules, this is too much. They can't seriously call this a slice of blackforest cake. It's transparent! And look at this cream. It's stale, and it came out of a can. It's fake cream, Jules. Fake.'

'It does appear to be canned whipped cream, I'll grant you that, but it tastes okay.'

'"Okay" isn't good enough, particularly when they're claiming to be the authentic, top drawer Austrian experi . . .' I froze in sudden horror. 'Jules—the cherries.'

'What about them?'

'They're . . . they're *glacé*. They've used glacé cherries instead of real ones, I mean goddammit Jules you can buy real cherries at any number of roadside stores. These people ought to be prosecuted under the Trade Practices Act.'

'Is there any chance you could stop complaining?'

'No. Ohmigod, have you tasted this coffee? It's *lukewarm*. This isn't happening.'

'Take it back then.'

'If I could catch a waiter's eye I would, but I see they can only afford blind waiters here.'

'You're really determined not to like the Blue Mountains, aren't you?'

'Do you blame me? This is appalling. I need real cream, real cherries, hot coffee and when I eat Austrian food I expect lots of it. Particularly when they have the gall to charge Double Bay prices. What are we paying for? The atmosphere? Ha!'

Rach and horses

So why are we going to the Blue Mountains? Because Jules wants to go horse-riding through the Megalong Valley, that's why. I will not be accompanying her. I don't like horses.

'You mean you're afraid of them.' Jules likes to keep her friends honest, but in this case she is not quite accurate. I'm not afraid of horses—I'm terrified of them. They have big teeth, big hooves, small brains and nervous constitutions. It's not a happy combination.

I did once try to be friends with a horsey girl at school. It was a brief moment in my teenage years when I thought I might branch out from life with the unutterably daggy kids in the drama club and see what the popular kids got up to. So I started hanging out with Tracy, the horse fancier. After a couple of weeks she took me to see her horse. Its name was Buttons, although apparently it was called Black Lightning when competing. Now, like Jules, I was a late developer—at fourteen, I was a very small, very skinny kid. Buttons looked about a hundred feet tall but Tracy called him 'sweety' and he ate a peaceful carrot so I began to think looks might be deceiving. We were there to groom him.

I started brushing one side and Tracy did his tail. She offered me the tail job but I though I'd stay out of range of his hind hooves. I was getting the hang of it when Tracy was called away by one of the trainers. Was I okay to keep going by myself? Sure I was. Actually I was kind of enjoying it, gently brushing this rather good-tempered animal. I was beginning to see why lots of girls liked horses. So Tracy left and I kept grooming. I finished my side and went around to do the other side, going via the head end, not the rear end, so as not to scare Buttons—see, I was learning the trade already. I felt quite proud. I started grooming the other side. Now, this side was near the wall. I was just getting into my swing when Buttons decided he had an itch to scratch and, apparently not noticing I was there, he rubbed himself against the barn wall. I was squished between the two, yelling for help. Buttons didn't realise that the yelling was coming from his ribs or, if he did, didn't care. He rubbed himself and me for all he was worth. That was the end for me and horses. I returned to the daggy kids in the drama club and spent the rest of my teen years indoors.

George, Mandy and the old nag

Only once more did I ever come face to face with a horse and that was when George and Mandy insisted I go horse-riding with them, against all my protests.

'You'll have fun!' they said.

'No, I won't,' I replied.

'Horses are great!'

'No, they aren't.'

'Riding's good for your soul!'

'No, it isn't.'

'Stop whining. You're going riding.'

'Wouldn't you rather play Scrabble?' I said. 'I'll let you wi-in.' But that only enraged them and they became more determined than ever.

On this occasion, they took me to a ranch in the Megalong Valley, the very one Jules is proposing to visit today. I kept up my bitter complaining but they ignored me (as my friends tend to when I complain). I told them that horse-riding was dangerous. They said 'rubbish'. I told them about the big teeth, small brain nexus. They said I was making a fuss about nothing. I told them about Buttons and my searing grooming incident. They said, 'Buttons—what a cute wittle name!'

I kept whinging but to no avail. When we got to the ranch, the first thing we saw was a giant sign—a truly enormous wooden sign. Written on it, in sky high capital letters, was this message:

HORSE-RIDING IS A DANGEROUS ACTIVITY. IF YOU ARE RIDING AT THIS RANCH, YOU DO SO AT YOUR OWN RISK. MANAGEMENT ACCEPTS NO RESPONSIBILITY FOR ACCIDENTS!!

'See? Look at that sign. Even the owners of the ranch agree with me. Turn this car around immediately, or we're all doomed!' They laughed and kept on going. Why does no-one take me seriously?

At the ranch, bow-legged, tough little men assessed our riding skills and matched us up with horses. We all saddled up: Mandy on a frisky colt, because she can actually ride; George on an equally frisky colt, because he's a bloke and didn't want to be upstaged by Mandy; and me on the sorriest, most broken down old nag the managers could find. The one they kept for the tiny tots out on their first ride. I was petrified. I was shaking. The horse gazed placidly at its surroundings. I tried to get it to go out the gate, but it was lost in thought and didn't seem to notice my pleas. The bow-legged saddler told me to say 'Giddup'. I squeaked out an approximation and the horse blew its lips out. George and Mandy were prancing outside the saddling pen, waiting for me.

The saddler said, 'Give 'er a kick.' I gave 'er a tentative nudge with my heel.

'No, a decent kick, lassie. Go on—you won't hurt 'er.'

I waggled my foot against her flank a bit harder and pleaded with her to move. She heaved a sigh, took a step forward, turned to her left, and went straight back into the barn where she stuck her nose in her feed bag.

'You've got to be firm with 'er,' said the saddler, sounding just a bit impatient, 'Show 'er 'oo's boss!'

'She knows who's boss,' I said, crossly. 'She is!'

George was laughing so hard he fell off his ride, so that was some consolation. I 'dismounted' and informed George and Mandy that I would be on the verandah, reading. 'Have a nice ride—I'll see you for tea'. And that was the last of horses for me.

👓 🍸 We meet an old friend

'Sure I can't tempt you with a ride?' Jules is the eternal optimist.

'Quite sure, thank you. I'll just park myself on this bench and watch the hippies flogging rubbish at inflated prices to the tourists.'

'Well, as long as you're going to enjoy yourself . . .'

'Hello, ladies.'

We looked up and there, large as life, was Folk Festival Girl. We greeted her enthusiastically, for we had fond memories of our drinkfest at the health retreat.

'Hello, you're just in time. Do you want to come horse-riding with me?'

'Can't stand horses, I'm afraid. Scared to death of them.'

'As are all sensible people,' responded Rach approvingly. 'I'll tell you the story of my only horse-riding trip.'

'Oh, lordy. Can you wait until I leave? I've heard this one a million times,' said Jules.

Rach turned to Folk Festival Girl. 'What are you doing today—do you want to join me for lunch? I have to wait here while Jules gets in touch with her wild side.'

'That'd be lovely. I'm not doing much. I was going to hitch a lift later this afternoon.'

'Where are you headed?' Jules asked. 'Maybe we can give you a lift.'

'Singleton. I've got cousins out there I'm going to visit.'

'I believe we can go Singleton way, can't we, Rach? We're heading to Lovedale ourselves.'

'Of course we can.' Rach had no idea where Singleton was. 'We'd love to.'

'Really? That'd be great. Do you have camping gear on you? I was going to camp out at Wollemi National Park tonight. Want to join me?'

'No,' said Jules.

'Yes,' said Rach. 'Jules, you owe me. We're going to two, count them *two* luxury resorts, so we have to have at least one decent camp.'

'If I must, I must.'

'You must.'

Rach turned to Folk Festival Girl: 'We'd love to come camping with you.'

Folk Festival Girl threw her arm around Rach. 'You're on.'

'And now, ladies,' said Jules, 'I'm going to leave you to your decadent lunching and spend a couple of hours with woman's best friend.'

✎ We skip the dull, repetitive bits and move right along to Jules' return

With that, Jules set off, and Folk Festival Girl and I settled down for lunch and a catch up. I gave her my views on the Blue Mountains and horse-riding since my mind was working along those lines and good stories always bear repeating. She agreed about the horses but, as she's a hippy herself, she was in two minds over the Blue Mountains. Yes, the Apple and Koala Claw Marinade is a disgrace, but look at the eucalypts!

Aren't they beautiful? Isn't this air crisp and clean? You can feel the oxygen coursing through your veins when you're out here. It makes you realise how glorious life is, doesn't it?

I let this flaw in her character pass and we got out a map of Wollemi National Park and had a lengthy debate on the best spot to camp. Dedicated campers always think they know the very best places to go and Folk Festival Girl and I were no exception. It's as well we didn't have to decide between sea camp and river camp or a blossoming friendship might well have been strangled at birth. The trouble is, we all have past paradises we want to recreate. I wanted to stay in a spot I'd been to fifteen years ago which I remembered fondly as one of the most magical campsites I'd ever found. She assured me that too many other campers had found it and now we'd have to share it with Christian Youth Groups— why spoil the memory? *She* wanted to go to a creek she knew of, but I am averse to creeks—they're unreliable. They dry up. One day it's a babbling brook, the next a mosquito-infested green trickle. Too risky. We let our fingers do the walking all over the map until we finally settled on a spot neither of us knew about, the great advantage being that if it turned out to be a dud no-one could be blamed.

With that settled, talk turned to the subject of tents and their rival merits, thermal bedrolls, sleeping bags we have known, and torches—when is big too big? It was late in the afternoon before Jules returned and we had barely touched on the important question of fire management techniques, but as these things bore Jules senseless we left that one for later and turned our attention to the returning hero.

🍷 Jules returns from her ride

'Howdy, pardner. Them's mighty purty bow legs ya got there,' said Rach, genially. 'How was your rahd?'

'Howdy, ladies. Ah jes' rode into town. Can an ol' cowpoke sit a spell?'

Folk Festival Girl begged us to cease with the cheesy Western accents.

'Sooooo, still alive then, I see,' said Rach. 'Did you have a good time?'

'It was great! Oh man, I haven't been on a horse in so long. I'd forgotten how wonderful it is to ride.'

'You're a good rider?' Folk Festival Girl was impressed.

'Jules was a State Junior Gymkhana champion.'

'The horse was terrific,' said Jules, 'a real goer, and the trail was beautiful. I feel wonderful.'

'What was the instructor like?'

Jules got a dreamy look in her eye. Uh oh.

'Jules?'

'Why are there so many gorgeous men in the world?' mused Jules. 'And why are they all gay?'

'He didn't respond to the Jules charm, then?'

'I gave it my best shot. You should have seen this one, Rach. Eyes to die for, and the way he handled his mount. Rrrrruff! He told me to ride next to him.'

Rach was instantly suspicious.

'He did, eh? That seems odd. Didn't he notice you were an expert rider?'

'I told him I hadn't been on a horse in a very long time,' said Jules airily.

'Jules! You didn't!'

'I did. I said I was feeling just a shade nervous.'

'You should be locked up, Jules. You and Lisa are a menace to society.'

'He asked me if I'd ridden much, and I said, "Um, a bit."'

'You didn't mention your dressage trophies, then.'

'He told me I should stay close to him until I found my rhythm.'

Folk Festival Girl spotted the flaw in J's strategy. 'What about when you wanted to run free. Didn't he notice your skill?'

'I toyed with the idea of pretending that my horse had run away with me so he could come galloping after and rescue me, but somehow . . .'

'Too complicated?'

'Yes. In the end it wasn't worth not galloping so I gave it away and just told him my nerves had steadied.' There was a slight pause, while Jules pondered whether to tell all, or not. 'I may also have said that riding is just like sex— you never forget how.'

'Did he fall off his horse?'

'Nearly. He managed to steady himself just in time, and then one of the beginner riders needed him, so I buzzed off for a serious ride. I let the wind sweep my hair, just in case.'

'What happened in the end?'

'Nothing. He smiled and was very sweet, but didn't make the slightest move.'

'Annoying.'

'Hm. Gay,' said Jules.

'Sydney. What can you do?'

We sat in silence for a while.

'Time to hit the road,' said Folk Festival Girl. 'We need to set up camp while it's still daylight.'

Jules groaned, 'I'd forgotten about camping.'

'I think it might be too late to set out tonight,' said Rach. 'Why don't we stay in the pub tonight and set off tomorrow?'

Jules immediately brightened. 'Stay in the pub? In a bed? With a pool table downstairs? Oh okay, if I must.'

'While we're there you can stock up on wine supplies for the camping we *will* be doing tomorrow,' said Rach. 'If you're pissed you may not notice you're sleeping in a tent.'

'Good idea. A few bottles of chardy, I think.' And Jules the wine buff set off for the pub in renewed high spirits. The men might all be gay or taken, but Australia still produces some of the finest wines in the world.

CHAPTER EIGHT

The Basil and The Boar

♟ A-camping we will go after Jules has visited the bottle shop

It's a funny thing about Rach—she won't get any fresh air, she hates exercise of any sort, she spends as much time as she possibly can indoors on her couch with her head buried in a book, but she adores camping. And here am I, the last of the outdoor girls, and I never go camping except when Rach insists on it. We've struck a deal this holiday, that I can go to luxury hotels as long as she can go camping at least once. I didn't put it in our itinerary in the hope that we'd 'run out of time', ahem, an old trick I picked up in the public service. If you don't want to discuss something, make sure you're the one setting the agenda for the meeting, and simply 'forget' to put it on the schedule.

But, since Folk Festival Girl had turned up unexpectedly and even more unexpectedly proffered the camping invitation, I didn't have the heart to protest, and certainly not when I saw Rach's face. There's nothing like sleeping with a rock in the middle of your back, being rained on and eaten by mozzies to cheer her up. And right now I'll do anything to get her off the subject of the Blue Mountains, even camp.

Luckily the bottle-o was fairly good (so it should be, according to Rach who says it supplies the local orthodontists with their drug of choice). I picked up two bottles of chardy and half a dozen reds to see me through the night. With all our luggage, we didn't have enough room in the car for Folk Festival Girl and her modest backpack, so I boxed up the winter coats, the wet weather gear and the EzyCook Fondue Maker (only $19.95 with a set of free fondue forks) I'd brought along for our Snowy Mountains trip and posted them home. That left room for our guest, some supplies for the night and a box of wine, with some extra space I'd be needing for my Hunter Valley purchases.

👓🍸 The girls commune with nature

In the car, we began with our customary music routine.

'What'll we have for road music, Rach?'

'What have we got in the CD box, Jules?'

'Hmmmm. *The Big Chill* . . . no . . . Kylie?'

'Don't really feel like Kylie. What about The Corrs?'

'For a journey starter? I don't think so.'

'I like The Corrs,' said Folk Festival Girl.

'But we need upbeat when we set out on the road,' objected Jules.

'I think we both know what we need, Jules.'

'Yes, I think we do, Rach.'

'ABBA!' we cried together.

'No!' cried Folk Festival Girl in alarm.

'Yes!' said Rach. 'And not just ABBA but . . . '

'"Dancing Queen"!' And despite Folk Festival Girl's vigorous protests nothing could stop the inevitable. The CD was in, the volume was up and we exhorted her to join in as we sang.

'*You* can dance! *You* can ji-ive . . . '

'No!'

'. . . *having* the time of your li-i-ife! Ooh ooh ooh . . . '

'Haven't you got something decent?'

' . . . *See* that girl! *Watch* that scene, diggin' the *dancing queen* . . .'

'I beg you for mercy!' shouted Folk Festival Girl above the thump of the ABBA beat. But it was no good. Once we are on a highway singing and doing the finger movements to 'Dancing Queen', not all your wit nor all your tears shall wash out a word of it.

When, finally, 'Dancing Queen' came to an end, we took pity on Folk Festival Girl and instead of launching into a spirited rendition of 'Rock Me', we switched to The Corrs.

'I deserve Bob Dylan after that,' said Folk Festival Girl.

'And we would gladly indulge you but we don't have anyone as soulful as Bob Dylan.'

'We've got Robbie Williams,' said Rach. 'At least he's got the same first name.'

'The Corrs will be fine.'

Having had our ABBA hit, we were happy to accommodate a guest. The conversation turned to the best spots to go camping in Wollemi National Park.

Jules got out her National Parks guide. 'It says here that there are three designated camping areas, all with showers, toilets and parenting facilities. I wonder what "parenting facilities" are?'

'Places where you can have unprotected sex, perhaps,' said Folk Festival Girl from the back seat.

'No such luck—it's a nappy changing table, according to the index. Ooh, the showers have hot water. This may not be so bad.'

Rach and Folk Festival Girl exchanged a look in the rearview mirror.

'Ah Jules, we're not camping in the designated camping area, mate.' Rach was firm.

'Why not? It has hot water.' Jules couldn't see the problem.

'Yes, and it also has four-wheel drives, small children and guitar-playing Swedish backpackers.'

'Rach is right,' said Folk Festival Girl. 'Designated camping areas are unspeakably awful.'

'So we're going to a lovely spot we found on the river,' said Rach.

'Ooh, where? I'll look it up,' said Jules flipping to the guide's index.

'Um, you won't find it in the guide, Jules. It's not an official camping site.'

'Is that legal?'

'Of course it's legal!'

'It says here that you can only camp in designated camping areas.' Jules was consulting the guide again.

'That's just a suggestion. It doesn't apply to experienced campers like us. As long as you observe fire safety so you don't start a bush fire, you're fine. Besides, the rangers can't cover the entire park in one night and they'll never find us in the place we're going to.'

'I thought you said this was legal,' said Jules.

'It is, it is. But sometimes the rangers can be a bit officious. They may not realise that we're experienced campers.'

'So it's not legal.'

'Not technically, no.'

'I don't think I'm comfortable breaking the law.' Jules thought she may have found a way to get her shower facilities after all.

'Forget it, Jules. We're not going anywhere near "facilities".'

The Eternal Mystery of Life

Camping is easy in Australia. Just find yourself a river bend, clear a spot for the fire, set up your tent, *et voilà!*—the perfect camp. Jules acceded to Rach and Folk Festival Girl in the matter of location and she had to agree that a secluded spot on the beautiful Colo River, with nothing around but the trees, the birds and the occasional kangaroo was better than sharing a parking lot with frisbee-playing kids and parenting facilities, even if she wasn't going to get a hot shower. Rach and Folk Festival Girl, both serious campers, set up their tents and started the fire. Jules volunteered to cook and opened a bottle of wine to get the party started.

'Chardy, Rach?'

'Don't mind if I do, Jules,' said Rach.

There was a short silence as Jules rummaged around in her provisions box. The silence became a touch frenzied as she dug herself into the box up to her armpits. Finally, she tipped the contents on the ground and in a burst of muttered curses, put each item back one by one.

'Jules,' said Rach finally, 'what *are* you doing?'

'I can't find the damned corkscrew! I brought everything else we need for a picnic—a grater, a tin opener, cutlery, picnic blanket, knives, fold-up table, insect repellent, salt, pepper, plastic cups, napkins, cutting board, plates, bowls, wine glasses. I've got everything we need except for the bleeping corkscrew. How could I have forgotten that of all things? *Now* what are we going to do? We can't open the bottles and I'm not doing this sober!'

A strange look passed over Rach's face. 'Just wait there.' she said. Going to the car, she opened the front door and took out her large handbag. With an eerie sense of the supernatural, she pulled out from its roomy interior . . . a corkscrew.

'I don't know why I put it in there,' she said dreamily. 'A force greater than myself moved my hand to the second drawer in the kitchen, and out it came. I just put it in, even though I knew you'd bring one along.'

We both stared at it.

'What does this mean?' asked Jules, 'Did the universe know I'd forgotten it?'

'Erm, she brought a corkscrew,' said Folk Festival Girl. 'What's odd about that?'

We looked at her. 'You don't understand. That's the *only* thing she brought.' We resumed gazing at the corkscrew.

'Ah well,' said Folk Festival Girl heartily, 'just as well it was the very thing we needed.'

For a spiritual girl, she was being strangely obtuse. That was the very point that had brought us face to face with the Eternal Mystery of Life forces. Rach *never* knows what's needed in any practical sense—how did she know we'd need the corkscrew? But then Jules realised that we could stand there contemplating infinity or she could open a bottle, so she opened the bottle and the three of us drank a toast to the outdoor life.

'I can't help thinking I've heard the name Wollemi National Park before,' pondered Jules.

'Probably. It's a reasonably well-known camping spot,' said Folk Festival Girl.

'No, not as a holiday destination. Something else. Something in history, or the news, and not something good, either.'

'It'll come back to you. What's for dinner?' asked Rach, turning to really important matters.

'Risotto, the perfect accompaniment to the chardy we are now enjoying.'

'Scrummo. Jules is an ace cook, as you will shortly appreciate,' said Rach. 'Jules, I've brought you an extra-thick rubber underlay and my best sleeping bag. There's a torch next to your bed, fly spray, a citronella candle and a sharp knife in case you need to kill a night-time intruder.'

Folk Festival Girl looked faintly astonished. Jules explained. 'I really don't take to camping. I get eaten by mozzies, even in the middle of winter. If there's a rock anywhere near our campsite, it'll find its way under my sleeping bag, and I'm frankly nervous of night-time noises. In the city, if I hear a car, I know it's a car. In the bush, I hear a rustle—well, it could be anything, couldn't it?'

'She can snuggle up to horses, but lizards send her running. Go figure. Come and check out your accommodation, J.'

'There's only one bed in here—where are you sleeping?'

'Outside. It's going to be a beautiful clear night, so I thought I'd sleep under the stars.'

'Getting close to nature?' said Folk Festival Girl, with a smile.

'Absolutely!'

'She had unhealthy influences in her youth,' said Jules. 'I should be thankful camping with her isn't even more primitive than this. Tell her about Pete the Pure, Rach.'

George Taxi, Pete the Pure and the Basil Incident of '94

George Taxi and I used to have a camping mate called Pete the Pure. At least, George and I called him Pete the Pure. This was on account of his very strongly held views on the correct way to camp. Pete thought that when you went camping, you should be as close to nature as possible. Not for Pete the eight-person family tent with dividing walls, automatic set-up, verandah and built-in fly screens. No, Pete the Pure slept under a canvas sheet flung over a low-hanging branch, pegged down by sticks he sharpened himself on site. And that's only if it was raining. If it was clear, he slept under the stars. No sleeping bag. He felt that the essence of camping was to put as little between you and nature as possible. Pete thought if you were going to camp in a luxury tent, you may as well book a room at the Hilton and spend your weekend watching in-house adult movies and calling room service. You certainly weren't communing with nature as far as Pete was concerned.

His views extended to camping paraphernalia. No briquettes allowed, only wood that you had collected yourself. No gas-powered stoves, no lights other than torches and matches, no fold-up tables, although he did allow fold-up chairs, but only the ones that have three-inch legs, so you're practically sitting on the ground. And he refused to allow his camping companions to ruin his experience by bringing along any of the above. George and I objected to the canvas tent flung over the branch, and there was a brief power struggle, but Pete the Pure gave our very simple tents the once-over and decided that, although borderline, they fell within the acceptably ascetic range.

Food was another matter on which Pete the Pure had strong views. It had to be plain and simple. Chops. Sausages. Not steak. No unnecessary condiments—salt only. Vegetables—only the most basic. Lettuce (iceberg, none of this cos or rocket stuff), tomato (no Tom Thumbs), cucumber (not Lebanese). This was particularly hard on George who loves cooking and is rather good at it. It's a lucky thing Pete was a very amusing guy and a good camper, because his demands were great.

In the summer of '94, the three of us decided to go camping in Kinchega National Park, which is on the western border of New South Wales. It's always fun driving across the flat plains west of the Great Dividing Range. Makes you realise how huge this country is. We took it easy and drove out over two days, camping under the stars at night.

Just outside Kinchega National Park is the tiny town of Menindee. 'Town' might be something of a misnomer as Menindee consists of one general store, selling, among other things, fresh and tinned food, camping gear, water, ice, petrol and tractor parts. We were there to buy our meat—with Pete supervising to make sure we stayed within prescribed culinary bounds. While Pete was discussing sausages with the lady behind the counter (I was still young enough to call all women over 40 'ladies'), George took a tour of the store to see if there was anything else we needed, and I sat on the front stoop trying to find a few good similes for a poem I was writing on inland Australia. Suddenly, I heard a sharp cry from inside the shop. It was George. He had broken into a joyous prance and was bounding toward us from the back of the store, waving something green in his hand.

'Basil!' cried George. 'I've found basil! I had no idea that you could get basil this far out of Sydney! This will be wonderful in a salad. I can make a bolognese, Hungarian style!'

Pete the Pure's face looked like a clap of thunder. Just as George danced up to the counter, basil and wallet in hand, Pete stepped between him and the cash register.

'We are not having basil,' said Pete in a quiet, yet authoritative, tone.

'What!? You can't be serious!' George was appalled. The idea of turning down a lucky find like this basil seared him to his soul.

'Basil is a luxury. We are here for the camping experience. We're not going on a gourmand's bus tour.'

'But it's basil! It's not exotic; it's just tasty.'

'*Tasty* is for city life, George,' said Pete, sententiously.

George drew a deep breath. 'That's what you really object to, isn't it. It's not about purity; it's about self-denial.'

'Yes, of course it's about self-denial. It's about getting back to nature's elements, not wallowing in Western decadence.'

'What's not natural about basil?' George's voice broke on a high note.

By this time, the boys were standing toe to toe and the atmosphere was tense. The lady behind the counter had been joined by what I guessed to be her two sons, a daughter with a baby and a decrepit old gent in a wheelchair, possibly the family's grandpa, all looking on in interest as two lads came to blows over a herb—a thing they rarely see in rugged outback Australia.

But George Taxi and Pete the Pure, although profoundly moved, each convinced of the rights of his case, were not prepared to kill for the cause. They decided to settle the matter with a push-up contest, held right there in the store. The rules were agreed upon.

'What counts as a push-up?' George let Pete make the call.

'A push-up is flat back and neck, chin and chest touch the floor at the down peak, shoulders and elbows level at the up peak. Rach, you're judge and counter. And don't let George cheat.'

The boys flattened to start position. The lady behind the counter handed me a whistle, and her brood gathered around. I blew the whistle and started the count.

'One . . . two . . . three . . . four . . .'

'YOUR CHEST DIDN'T TOUCH THE FLOOR.' Pete the Pure lived up to his name.

'George, you must do them properly,' I said. 'Start again on my whistle.'

'One . . . two . . . three . . . four . . .'

Now, we were on the edge of the Australian desert in the middle of summer. It was very hot that day—40 degrees in the shade and humid with it. After five push-ups, the boys were sweating badly.

'. . . eleven . . . twelve . . . thirteen . . .'

'Are you going far?' the lady behind the counter asked me, her eyes glued to the two straining men on the floor.

'Nah, we're just staying in Kinchega, then back to Sydney . . . eighteen . . . nineteen . . . twenty . . .'

'Have you got enough ice?'

'Ooh. We forgot all about the ice . . . twenty-three . . . twenty-four . . . We'll take two bags . . . twenty-six . . .'

'Larry, get the ice out of the fridge.' Larry reluctantly dragged himself away.

'. . . thirty . . . thirty-one . . . Actually make that four bags, I think the boys are going to need extra . . . thirty-four . . . thirty-five . . .'

'Larry can put it in the car for you. Larry!'

'. . . thirty-eight . . . thirty-nine . . . Would you? Thanks Larry . . . forty-one . . .'

'Pleasure.'

'. . . forty-three . . . forty-four . . . How much all up? . . . forty-five . . .'

'That'll be fifteen dollars for the snags and the ice.'

'. . . forty-six . . . Best not add the basil just yet,' and I handed her a twenty.

'Ta love,' and she rang up the till, took out a five and handed it to me, all without taking her eyes off the battle in front of her.

'. . . forty-nine . . . fifty . . . thanks . . . fifty-one . . . fif . . .'

With a cracking groan, George collapsed on the floor. Pete struggled out one more perfect push-up, just to make sure the contest was his, and fell, panting, next to George. They lay on the floor staring at the ceiling, both of them exhausted, their clothes more sweat than cotton. The store owners burst into polite applause. After a few minutes, Pete rolled onto all fours and heaved himself to his feet.

'I win. No basil.'

And with that, he picked up the sausages and exited the store. George stayed where he was for a few seconds, then staggered to his feet.

'How much for the basil?' he asked the lady behind the counter.

'Three dollars fifty a bunch.'

'Sold.'

And he hid it in his pants. I made a mental note not to eat the Hungarian bolognese.

⌐◯ Y The homesick ranger and the wild boar

'I take it Pete the Pure didn't like designated camping sites either,' said Jules.

'Of course not! No, we stayed in a beaut spot right on the lake. We had to pass a sign telling us Do Not Proceed. I remember we debated the point and then decided that since we had come so far it would be criminal to be held back by a wooden board with a bit of paint on it. That was the only time I've ever been bailed up by a ranger.'

'Ooh,' said Jules, 'maybe we'll be interrogated by a ranger tonight!'

'Did he move you on?' asked Folk Festival Girl.

'He tried to, the poor sap, but two things happened. One, he fell for the Rach charm—I was wearing a miniskirt, ahem—and two, it turned out he was desperately lonely, hated living in the middle of nowhere and pined for Sydney. I swear, when we said we were from Sydney his face lit up and he begged us to tell him all about home. How was Glebe? Had we been to the Valhalla lately? Did we ever go to Oxford Street on a Saturday night? Luckily, Pete the Pure and George Taxi were both party animals so they brought him up to date on the Sydney scene. I did my bit by being eye candy and gazing at him as though I might, if he played his cards right, fall in love with him.'

'Subtle,' said Jules.

'Thanks,' said Rach. 'We said we were glad to be out of the place for a couple of days and the only thing we missed was decent coffee. It turned out the ranger had brought truckloads of coffee beans and a cappuccino machine with him when he was exiled to Menindee. The boys were ecstatic.'

'I thought Pete the Pure wanted to get back to nature,' said Jules. 'Unless it's made of bark, I fail to see how a cappuccino machine is part of the rugged outdoor life.'

'George and I thought the same, but Pete said coffee is different, and since George was desperate to get a real cap, he let it go.'

'So what happened then?'

'We showed him that our fire was well out of range of any eucalypts and he agreed to let us stay in our spot. He did, however, warn us of a wild boar that was roaming the park.'

'There are *wild boar* in our National Parks?' cried Jules.

'There are wild boar in *some* National Parks,' said Rach.

'Are they in this one?'

Rach restrained herself from teasing her. 'No, they are not in this one.'

'How do you know?'

'Because I just know, that's how. If there were you'd hear them in the bush. And we don't hear them.'

'They might be in other parts of the park, just waiting for us to go to sleep!' Jules had a new worry to add to her list.

'Well, they're not,' said Rach.

'Seriously, Jules,' said Folk Festival Girl, 'I've never seen a wild boar in our parks and I camp all the time.'

Jules sighed in relief.

'Oh right, so you believe her, but not me,' said Rach, indignantly.

'That's because you'd tell me anything rather than camp where there's a proper toilet.'

Rach had to admit that was right.

'So keep telling us about the ranger. Did you get your coffee?' Folk Festival Girl steered us back to the story.

'We set up camp first, made dinner . . .' began Rach.

'What did Pete the Pure let you have for dinner?' Jules likes all the details.

'Sausages. George made them, and I thought I caught a hint of basil. I saw a suspicious look cross Pete's face, but he said nothing. How could he, after exposing his gourmet coffee underbelly? But they were just a bit too delicious to be unseasoned snags. I tried to forget where the basil had been.

'Anyway, it was getting dark, and Pete and George really wanted a good after-dinner coffee. I like coffee, too, but I'd had enough of the ranger's company, so I was happy to let them go by themselves; that way I could enjoy a few hours' peace reading and tending the fire. They chivalrously got me a blanket from the car so I wouldn't freeze, put another log on the fire, then took the car and set off into the night. Meanwhile, I settled down into my chair and started to read my murder mystery. I'd only got a few pages in when I heard a sound that made my blood freeze—the mighty *Maooooooooooooooo* of a wild boar, followed by the sounds of a giant pig crashing through the bush. My heart stopped. Outside the firelight, the bush was completely black— I couldn't see a thing. I could hear the boar rampaging through the undergrowth, roaring now and then, but I couldn't tell how close it was. It sounded like it was going to crash right into my chair any minute. I had no car, so no protection and no means of escape. All I could do was sit in my chair, huddled in my blanket, praying to God that He'd spare my life. I thought, "Surely the boys will hear the boar and come back to rescue me."'

'But they were at the ranger's.'

'Yes, and I couldn't remember whether the ranger's hut was near or far. They'd shown me the map, but I must say I wasn't paying any attention, so I had no idea when they were likely to be back. I had to wait in terror for what seemed like hours. There were occasional bouts of silence when I thought maybe the wild boar had gone away, and then the snorting and crashing would begin again. I kept telling myself that I was imagining its proximity, that it was really miles away and the sound was carrying on the wind. But it was no good—it got so every rustle had me jumping out of my skin. I've never been so relieved as when I heard the car and saw the headlights.

'As they got out of the car, I rushed up and flung myself on them, shouting, "Aaaaarghhhh, thank God you're back. The wild boar's somewhere near this campsite—I'm sure of it. I've been hearing it grunting and crashing ever since you left!" I thought they'd tell me that I must have imagined it, but instead they were silent. Suspiciously so. Pete would have maintained silence, but George can't lie about anything.

'"We know," he said. "As we were driving away, it crossed the track right in front of us. We nearly crashed into it."

'"You what!? You nearly ran into it and you *left me here alone*?" I was furious.

'"We thought about coming back but I really wanted a

cappuccino," said Pete, apparently thinking that would explain it all perfectly.'

'You're kidding me!' said Folk Festival Girl.

'That's what I said. "We knew you'd be all right," said George, trying to unwrap my hands from around Pete's neck, "You're more than a match for a wild boar."

'And since I *was* all right, I let it go. I asked them whether the coffee had been worth risking a dear friend's life and they said that it had been. The ranger had been palpably disappointed not to see my lovely face on his doorstep, only the somewhat less lovely Pete and George, and at first he didn't want to let them in. But Pete was determined and the ranger gave way. Then he tried to fob them off with instant coffee, and again Pete was forced to assert his will. So they got their coffee and in return they regaled the ranger with descriptions of Sydney. Apparently, the poor man's hut was plastered with photos and posters of the big smoke. Not a sign of anything to do with the bush. Once he closed his door on his day's work, he didn't want to think about the damned bush, he just wanted to dream of the day he could escape all this quiet and once more live in the centre of the universe—Sydney.'

'Did you hear the wild boar again?'

'Yes, but going in the general direction of away, so we didn't let it bother us. Besides, we had the car, so we had some protection and a means of escape should we need it.'

CHAPTER NINE

Night under the stars

👓 🍸 **We open a few bottles . . .**

By the time Rach got to the end of her story, the first bottle
was finished so Jules opened a second chardy and a red
she'd brought along as an after dinner treat, 'to let it breathe'.
We had finished dinner and were sitting around the campfire
under the Milky Way. It was by now quite dark and poor
Jules kept seeing shadows move in the bushes.

'I wish I could remember where I've heard the name
"Wollemi National Park" before,' said Jules. 'It's really
annoying me.'

'Why do you need to remember?' asked Folk Festival Girl.

'I keep feeling there's something important about it, and
I need to remember what, but I just can't put my finger
on it.'

'Say,' said Folk Festival Girl, changing the subject, 'I was going to ask you two if either of you has tried an internet dating service.'

'Yeah, I have,' said Jules (well, what did you expect, that Rach would?). 'Why do you ask?'

'Erm, well, against my better judgement I signed on to RSVP.com. A friend of mine insisted—she thinks I don't make enough effort to find a partner. Can't say I ever thought it would be a good idea.'

'Me either,' said Rach. 'I always suspected that RSVP.com would be a dud. Who are all these bubbly people who like dining out and romantic walks on the beach? And if there are so many of them, how come we can all quote every line of "Seinfeld"?'

'Did it work for you, Jules?' asked Folk Festival Girl.

'Depends on your definition of "work". If you mean did I find a partner, then obviously, no, but if you mean did I find a bunch of sad, scarred men I would accompany only to the nearest mental home then, yes, it worked a treat.'

'That bad, huh.'

'They tell me that some people have found their true love over the net. I have yet to meet one.'

'How many guys did you meet?'

'Two.'

'Only two? You give up easy, Jules,' said Folk Festival Girl. 'You have to give it more than just two dates.'

'Oh, these didn't get as far as dates,' said Jules. 'Good heavens, no. Although I did get as far as a phone call with the first one. His name was Darren. Or Dazza, as he liked to be called. Which reminds me of a poem Lisa once wrote when we were living in Bathurst. Being a country town, Bathurst was full of people called Dazza and Bazza and Shazza. One Christmas, Lisa rewrote the words to a verse of 'Twas The Night Before Christmas' using all the names of our friends and lovers and we went around reciting:

> And he whistled and shouted and called them by name:
> Now Dazza! Now, Bazza! Now, Shazza and Stretch!
> On Cardo! On Blotto! On Dicko! And Fletch!
> Get the dope from the pub, don't stumble or fall,
> Now hash away, hash away, hash away all!

'Didn't your friends and lovers object?' asked Rach.

'We only recited it to each other. It was like a secret handshake.'

'So what happened with your RSVP Dazza?' asked Folk Festival Girl.

'He seemed okay on the email so I agreed to a phone call. I sent him my mobile number and 30 seconds later, he called. Straightaway, Dazza made it clear that he was not interested in a relationship by using the time-honoured phrase, "I'm in it for the sex."'

'A poetic man, then,' said Folk Festival Girl.

'All class,' said Rach.

'Quite,' said Jules. 'No subtlety about our Dazza. But, as you know, I'm in it for the sex too, under certain conditions. If I'm going to have to chew my arm off in the morning, it's just not worth it, but I'm definitely in the market for a decent lover, so I got him talking about himself. Oh dear, is all I can say about that.'

'Arm chewer?'

'And how. He started by telling me that he had had 150 lovers from RSVP.'

'You should have asked for a reference,' said Folk Festival Girl.

'No need,' said Jules. 'His next sentence lost him the job. He told me that his favourite position is doggy style. Am I the only person who thinks that phrase should be canned? It's so ugly. As soon as he said it I knew he was out of the question—it's not the position I object to, it's the name. He carried on for a bit about his technique and his success with women, and I listened politely . . .'

'As you do,' said Rach.

'As you do. I think he guessed that he was losing the sale, because then he offered to send me a picture of his penis.'

'No!' Folk Festival Girl was agog.

'Yes. I politely declined, thanked him for his call and rang off. He called a few more times, leaving dirty messages in the hope that I'd be persuaded to change my mind, but somehow, don't ask me how, I always managed to resist.'

'What about the second one?' asked Folk Festival Girl.

'Ooh, this is a good one,' said Rach. 'I was there when she got his email. In fact, do you know, Jules, I think I still have it in my notebook.' Rach keeps a notebook of ideas for her poetry. She rummaged about in her now fabled Eternal Mystery of Life bag.

'I've kept it for a satirical sonnet on modern life I'm composing for the university's student mag. Here it is. Wait 'til you read this,' said Rach to Folk Festival Girl.

Jules:

thanks for replying. to be honest, i didn't think you would reply. you are the first lady who has replied to me after seeing my photo. i would like to ask you some questions. you are not on any medication or substance, are you? (just teasing)

'I'm not,' said Jules, 'but now he comes to mention it, there's an open bottle here—chardy, Rach?'

'Don't mind if I do, Jules.'

there are over 260,000 profiles on rsvp site, what made you to select my profile. you know, my profile name is compulsive liar,

'He didn't really call himself *Compulsive Liar*, did he?' Folk Festival Girl couldn't believe it.

'Oh, yeah,' said Jules.

i have said, i am short, fat, ugly and unemployed and didn't have a pics on my profile? i would really appricate if you could tell me, the motive for selecting a short, fat, ugly, compulsive liar out of that many good looking, financially secure, honest, and genuine profiles?

'Actually, that's a good question, Jules, why *did* you reply to this guy?'

'Desperation.'

my second question is about your profile, you said you are looking for short term relationship or long term relationship. i did go to school but i never paid any attention to english or maths. what do you mean by short term relationship. do u mean one night stand. i am sorry to ask you these questions but i want to understand what is happening in your mind. i don't think any man would be able to understand what does a woman think, but if you give me some explaination, i might see the what you have been thinking at that time.

'We are all wondering that, my friend,' said Rach.

in other word, i want to find out the real reason for your to join rsvp site? i have been on streets and have seen that it is much easier for ladies to find someone than it is for guys. if you are looking for short term relationship, all you have to do, is to go to your local pub.

'Tried that,' said Jules.

my third question is about your job, i am not as educated as you are. i hated school. the only thing i liked about school was lunch breaks, but i am street wise and i learned my lessons on streets.

'He mentions streets a lot, doesn't he?' said Folk Festival Girl.

the other think is about your photo, i don't really care about how people look outside, i beleive the beauty is within people and it takes time to find that, the reason, i like to see your picture is to put a face to your words. i had been married once, i have her

photos and happy to send to you, she is model. very
beautiful but no personality.

'We were wondering whether it was Elle or Claudia he was
referring to,' said Jules. 'They've both recently broken up with
a lover.'

i have been single for last five years and can not find
any lady who is confident and genuine and honest
with herself. they don't have to be honest with me.
at least they could be honest with themseleves. what
is important to me is personality not look, personality
will stay for ever but old age will take the facial beauty.
i hope you can find the photo out of your magazines
sooner than later.

'What's that "magazine" stuff, Jules? Did he think you were
a model?'

'I have *no* idea. Poor man's suffering terrible delusions
and that's just one more to add to his list.'

i am not sure what to say about myself. would you
believe a guy with profile name and email address
compulsive liar? are u sure you arenot on any
medications?

'Regrettably, no,' said Jules. 'Medication might be fun.'

ask any questoins you want and i will tell you the
truth. the whole truth. by the way innocent until
proven guilty.
i should mention i have very good sense of humour
and i hope to hear from you again.

When we got to the end of this little missive we reached for another bottle and contemplated the last sentence. Somehow it was both funny and sad.

'So how far did *you* get?' asked Jules of Folk Festival Girl. 'Did you meet anyone?'

'I had a look at a lot of profiles,' said Folk Festival Girl. 'And most I left alone on the strength of their RSVP name.'

'Oh, I know what you mean,' said Jules, 'like LatinLoverBoy and HornyGuy, or—my personal favourite—StrapMe.'

'StrapMe?' Rach was appalled. 'The mind boggles.'

'Exactly. What are those people thinking?' said Folk Festival Girl. 'So weeding out the no-goes was easy. In fact, I only came across one I thought might suit me. He was into alternative therapy and crystals, a musician, a vegetarian . . .'

'Sounds like he should be locked up immediately,' said Rach.

'To me, those qualities were pluses.'

'I suppose it takes all sorts,' Rach didn't sound very convinced.

'Rach, let her finish.'

'Anyway, we emailed back and forth, and you know how it is when you're just emailing—it can seem so right. He liked everything I liked. He even said he liked camping. We had one phone call. We didn't talk for long, I forget why, I think I was up to my eyeballs in work, but long enough for me to start thinking he might be The One. He had a beautiful voice.'

'That's always a killer,' agreed Jules.

'So for our first date, I went to meet him at his place.

I turned up at the appointed hour only to be greeted by his mother . . .'

'He lived with his mother?' Rach thought Folk Festival Girl should have left then and there.

'Yes, and it was she who answered the door. I stuck out my hand to say hello but she ignored it, came out onto the porch, closed the door behind her, hustled me to the edge of the porch as far away from the house as she could, and in a hurried whisper said to me, "Watch out for my son. He'll steal from you."'

'I rest my case,' said Rach.

'I didn't have time to explore this with the mother because she said that one sentence, dashed back indoors, *closed the door*, then opened it again and said in a hearty, welcoming voice, "Come in, my dear, come in. We've been so looking forward to meeting you."

'I was startled but I reasoned that anyone might have a mad mother and still be quite normal—I thought of my own dear mother and how she might appear to people unused to her quirks. So I went on the date despite the dodgy gene pool.'

'And I take it he was not normal?'

'No. Not even remotely. Wore his pants up around his armpits. Socks with sandals at night. Who the mad one might be—him or his mother or both—was not something I ever discovered. He talked about a Dungeons and Dragons game he and a net friend had been playing for the last four years. He did have a crystal collection—he shared it with his mother, who was a witch, apparently. One date was plenty.'

'And did he steal from you?'

'Didn't get the chance. I took one look at him and superglued myself to my purse.'

'What's so strange about internet dating services,' said Jules thoughtfully, 'is how everyone describes themselves as slim, bubbly, financially sound and into travel and fine living, when they are really unfit, emotionally stunted couch potatoes—just like us, in fact.'

We stared into the fire, drinking a very decent shiraz and contemplating a world filled with lunatics, ourselves most probably included. Jules opened another bottle and we wondered what a truthful internet dating ad would look like. Here's what we came up with.

Jules:

Career bureaucrat badly scarred by history of disastrous singles events and desperate to break a long, long drought seeks Mr Perfect. Must have no flaws whatsoever. GSOH essential. One-night stands considered.

Rach:

Easily irritated, neurotic woman in her mid 30s who can't bear walks on the beach or fine dining seeks brooding artist trapped in soul-destroying job. Alcoholism okay.

Folk Festival Girl:

Independently minded Pisces seeks soul mate to share good times and crystal collection. Must be open to alternative therapy, vote Green and have verifiable history of street protest activities. Leos need not apply.

And that cheered us up. No wonder we were all single. One more glass and we were ready for bed. Rach stretched out on her sleeping bag next to the fire, Folk Festival Girl and Jules retired to their tents, and silence fell on our campsite.

Y Jules remembers where she's heard the name before

I lay in my sleeping bag on the extra thick rubber mattress trying to find the least lumpy position, which was no easy matter. If this was the extra thick mattress, what was the thin one like? How could anyone sleep under these conditions? I lay on my side, then on the other side, then on my back, then back to the first side. I tried curling up both knees, one knee, then dead straight. It made no difference. Like the princess of the fable, I felt like I was sleeping on a pea, only this was the Australian version and there were hundreds of packets of frozen peas under my bed, all of them digging into my sensitive bits. I was on my back saying Ohm on every out breath, when all of a sudden I heard a snuffling sound. I froze. I lay totally still and stopped breathing so I could identify the noise. There it was again but louder this time! My heart was thumping against my chest. Silence. Then I heard a rustle followed by a loud gurgling growl, and there was no question about it— whatever it was was right in our camp and it was huge! Oh my God, it's a wild boar! I sat up in bed and reached for my knife. I was just about to shout out to the girls, when the snuffle-rustle-gurgling growl sequence was repeated.

I paused. There it went again. And then I realised what the boar-like sounds were. Rach was snoring loud enough to rattle the gum trees. Amazingly, Folk Festival Girl slept on undisturbed.

In incredible relief, I collapsed back down on the mattress, jarring my spine on a sharp rock that had found its way under my tent. I scrabbled around vainly trying to move it out from under me, but nothing would dislodge it, so I had to move the entire mattress until it was jammed up against the side of the tent. In this way, as long as my legs were bent into a diamond shape and I lay on my side at an angle of 60 degrees, I managed to avoid all the larger lumps under the mattress. I breathed deeply, recalling the difficult sleeping positions yogis imposed upon themselves, far more irritating than this one, and still they slept soundly so I could too. I pictured myself sleeping, sleeping, floating on a cloud, being massaged by the riding instructor, oops, better not go there, no back to the floating, floating . . .

I was just dropping into a light doze when I heard the dread sound: *Zzzzzzz*. No, not a snoring variant from Rach (her symphony continued outside, but I had almost erased it from my consciousness), but a mosquito. And a big one from the sounds of it. I tried to bury myself under the sleeping bag but I could still hear it. There was nothing for it but to turn on the torch and apply the fly spray. Of course, as soon as the torch went on, the mozzie ducked for cover and stopped buzzing. It was to be a battle of attrition then. I turned off the torch and waited. In seconds the buzzing started again. Torch on, silence. Torch off, *Zzzzzzz*. This went on for a few minutes before I finally trapped it in a corner and put an end to its little life. I was a fraction too enthusiastic with the Mortein, though, and managed to smoke myself out of my own hole. I needed to wee anyway so, coughing, I crawled out of the tent. There was just enough firelight for me to see Rach sleeping like a baby, not even a net covering her, apparently untroubled by mosquitoes and rocks and snoring loud enough to set off car alarms in Sydney. I bitterly contemplated the unfairness of it all and uncorked the last bottle. A glass of wine should put me to sleep.

Back in my tent after my nightcap, I took up the diamond-leg-60-degree-angle position and tried again. It was no good. The bush is full of strange noises—whispers and crackles and furry rustlings—and at every suspicious sound my eyes would fly open, blood pounding in my veins, as I waited to see which sharp-toothed carnivore was trying to break into my tent to snack on me. I had finally managed to slip into a light doze—that state you are in just before going properly to sleep—and my mind was playing over the events of the day: the wafer thin blackforest cake, the horse ride, the campfire, the RSVP ads, when suddenly a terrible memory smashed into my brain and I sat up and screamed.

'Jesus, Jules—is that you? What's the matter?' Folk Festival Girl sounded alarmed.

I was in a cold sweat.

'I've remembered where I heard the name before— Wollemi National Park. It was the Backpacker Murders! This is where all the backpackers were killed!'

'Jules,' Rach sounded as patient as a short-tempered woman woken suddenly from a deep sleep can sound, 'that was Belanglo National Park.'

'It was?'

'Yes.'

'Oh.'

'It's a pretty park. We can pay it a visit, if you like,' said Rach.

'No, that's okay.'

There was silence as we all settled back into our beds.

'Rach?'

'Yes?'

'I'm never coming camping again.'

'Fair enough. Night, Jules.'

Jules' ordeal comes to an end

Although I was certain that I would stay awake all night, the next thing I remember is waking to the sounds of splashing. The sun was up and I could hear the girls messing about outside. I unravelled myself from the sleeping bag, unzipped the tent and went out to greet the new day. Rach was in the river, having a morning bath. Naked, of course. Pete the Pure didn't believe in bathing suits, either. She has often told me about her love of this ritual—the morning dip in a freezing river followed by coffee at the campfire.

'Hello, there,' said Folk Festival Girl, cheerily. She was sitting cross-legged by the fire, tending a couple of pieces of toast. 'Sleep all right?'

Before I could answer this outrageous accusation, Rach hailed me from the river.

'Jules, baby! Come on into the water. It's marvellous in here. It'll make the whole trip worthwhile.'

I cautiously made my way to the bank, which sloped gently down into the river. It was dark brown, smelly, and an experimental toe told me it was also squishy and slimy. God knows what was waiting in the mud to nibble on my toes.

'No thanks. I think I'll stay right here. Did you know there are eels in this river?'

Rach grinned. 'Is that revenge for last night?'

'I can't think what you mean,' I replied innocently.

'The eels are okay; it's the river snakes you have to watch out for.'

I leapt back from the river's edge and Rach roared with laughter, the cow. That was it for me. I packed up my things, stowed them in the car and spent the rest of the morning on Rach's camping chair reading Patricia Cornwell. When Rach got out of the river she sensed I needed soothing so she asked me, kindly, if I'd had any sleep at all last night.

'About two hours, I'd say, and that was despite all the noise, both bush and human.'

'Oops, I snored, did I? Was it very loud?'

'Only slightly louder than an enthusiastic maracas band at the Rio Carnivale.'

'Sorry about that, chief,' said Rach.

'That explains my recurring dream last night,' said Folk Festival Girl. 'We were in the middle of the San Francisco earthquake and we couldn't escape. The ground was heaving under our feet.'

'That was just Rach sending shock waves through the earth.'

'It's only really bad when I've had too much to drink.'

'Strangely I think you might be right, Jules,' said Folk Festival Girl. 'I had the same dream when we all slept in my room after our party at the retreat.'

'There you go.'

'Jules, did I tell you that Thelma has taken to sleeping with her head on the pillow next to mine?'

'Oh, that's so cute!' I was momentarily cheered by this picture.

'You'd think, wouldn't you? But the bad news is—she snores. Seriously. She keeps me awake all night. What with that and demanding to be let out or in every five minutes, I'm as wearied as a mother with a newborn babe. You know, if I'd bitten the bullet twelve years ago and got married and had children instead of taking on Thelma, the kids would be old enough to let themselves out at night by now and I could have divorced my snoring husband. But no, I had to get a cat.'

'Do you good,' I said unsympathetically.

'You haven't had enough sleep,' said Rach, 'or you wouldn't be so grumpy. Why don't you snuggle down in the backseat and get some shuteye on the way to Singleton?'

'Who's going to navigate?'

'I'll take on that task,' said Folk Festival Girl.

Rach was right. I needed a nap to recover from the terrors of the night. So, while Folk Festival Girl guided Rach out of the park, I curled up on the back seat, put on my favourite sleeping mask—midnight blue with a yellow moon and white stars—and drifted off. The last thing I heard was Folk Festival Girl saying to Rach, 'Aren't we going to Singleton?'

'Yes.'

'We should have turned left, then, not right.'

I had forgotten to warn her that the navigator has to tell Rach *everything*. You can't rely on her reading signs. Not to worry, we'd get there eventually, and I fell into a deep sleep.

Incredibly, even though I hadn't organised a step-by-step map complete with journey times, we made it to Singleton, where we deposited Folk Festival Girl after fond farewells and an exchange of numbers and email addressess. As we turned onto the main road out of Singleton, Rach and I agreed that we'd rarely met a more decent specimen, with only one flaw that we could see—an unhealthy dislike of ABBA. Speaking of which . . .

'I think it's time for highway music, don't you Rach?'

'Took the words right out of my mouth, Jules. What'll we have?'

We smiled at each other and soon the car rang to our merry voices: '*You* can dance! *You* can ji-ive! *Having* the time of your li-i-ife! Ooh ooh ooh! *See* that girl! *Watch* that scene, diggin' the *dancing queen* . . .'

CHAPTER TEN

Jules gets very drunk

 Rach meets Jules' relatives

Jules cheered up amazingly after her nap and our ABBA singalong. Our next destination was the Glengarrie Park Bed & Breakfast at Lovedale, in the heart of the Hunter Valley wine district, run by Jules' brother-in-law's parents, Janice and Bob. We got to their B&B in the late afternoon. Jules was thrilled to be back in civilisation and in the bosom of her very lovely family. For once we were in complete accord on the accommodation. We had a room each, with an ensuite that looked like my old Gran's bathroom—huge with a lion-foot bath, carved wooden cabinets and blue and white tile patterns.

Look up 'mein host' in the dictionary and I bet it says 'Janice and Bob Oxenbould'. I've never met two more gregarious people. Janice kissed us both, shepherded us into their huge country kitchen, put out the coffee, tea and biscuits and settled in for a long overdue gossip about old friends and family with Jules. The air was soon filled with No! Did she? I don't believe it! Did you hear what happened to Will? Mongolia!? Not only that, he said it to her brother! And so on. They had a marvellous time catching up on the news and recalling old scandals.

While they were yacking, I drifted off into my own world. The house and garden were so warm and beautiful it was easy to sink into contemplation of a possible pastoral ode. I was mentally flipping through my pathetically small list of known flowers to see if I could find a decent country rhyme— daisy/hazy, rose/glows, lily/billy, anemone/Philharmoni-c— when my attention was caught by the conversation. Jules was talking about someone called Ridge. Apparently he'd slept with his best friend's girlfriend, the cad. But 'Ridge'? That seemed an odd sort of name. Jules' parents are called Reg and Joan, her sisters are Kerry, Sue and Pam. Who could this Ridge be? And then Jules said 'What about Macy?' And Janice said, 'I *know*, can you believe it?'

At that moment, Bob walked in and said, 'What about Macy?'

'She's in a coma!' said Jules, excited.

'Yay!' shouted Bob. 'I can't stand Macy.'

Well, there are black sheep in every family, but I couldn't help thinking that poor old Macy seemed to have drawn the popularity short straw.

'Jules read the latest *TV Soap*. She can tell us everything,' said Janice.

Bob pulled up a chair. 'What's Brooke going to do? Is she leaving Ridge?'

Ah, the mystery solved itself. I had fallen into a family of soap addicts. 'The Bold and the Beautiful' is their favourite, followed by 'Days of Our Lives', or, as they are known to soap freaks, 'Bold' and 'Days'.

We dine at the bed & breakfast

Bob and Janice insisted that we dine with them the first night, to feed us up for our gruelling tour of the wine district the next day. Bob was making a lamb roast.

'I'm great at cooking lamb,' said Bob, 'and I'm terrific with roast potatoes and steamed spinach. It's time I have a problem with. So we may be having excellent roast lamb and raw potatoes, or possibly crispy roast veg and burnt roast. Or, we may be lucky, and everything will be ready at the same time. I never know.'

'Oh, Bob. Don't be silly,' said Janice. 'Have you put the roast on yet?'

'No. No, I can't say I have.'

'Bob, it's six thirty! Put the roast on.'

'Right. I'll be back. Everyone right for a drink?'

Dinner went for seven hours and even Rach, who normally can't take more than two hours of anyone's company, let alone people she doesn't know well, didn't want to go to bed at the end of it. We started by discussing sex, as you do. Janice had to tell Jules about a development in the life of a young friend of theirs.

'Kay told me she's come to an arrangement with Alan, now she's produced all the kids they want. They won't have sex anymore. It turns out she can't bear it. She likes him all right, but not sex, and she'd rather he get it elsewhere and not bother her anymore.'

'But what if he falls in love with someone else?'

'No fear of that, Kay says. She's far too good a cook and he loves the kids, so . . .'

'So . . . what? Prostitutes?'

'Ooh, I didn't think to ask. I assumed he'd just do what they all do and sleep with his secretary.'

'Oy!' exclaimed Bob.

'Sorry, dear. Not you of course.'

'Amazing. It's such a nineteenth century thing to do.'

'Isn't it though? Most people would get therapy, but not Kay. She just says that's the way she is and she's not bothered as long as Alan isn't.'

'And is he?'

'Apparently not. He's agreed to it. Probably already sleeping with his secretary.'

From there we ranged over strange marriages, then film stars' strange marriages, then other habits of film stars.

'I'll tell you something that will astound you,' said Bob. 'Did you know that Jennifer Lopez employs a Nipple Tweaker?'

We expressed amazement.

'It's true. There really is someone whose job it is to tweak J. Lo's nipples. It's for when she's having her picture taken. The cameraman sets it up, Jennifer gets into her pose, everything's ready for the shot except her nipples aren't as perky as they could be. That's when the Nipple Tweaker steps in . . .' Bob illustrated with hand movements on an imaginary J. Lo, '. . . and tweaks her nipples. She's got a Bottom Watcher, too.'

'What does the Bottom Watcher do?' Rach loves people like Bob.

'I'm glad you asked. It's a complicated job. The Bottom Watcher has to check that she has no panty line showing in the shot. He comes in at the same time as the Nipple Tweaker.'

'Couldn't the Bottom Watcher and the Nipple Tweaker be the same lucky person?' asked Jules.

'Oh, no, no, no,' said Bob. 'They're two very different skill sets. One needs an eagle eye, the other a dextrous thumb and forefinger. You wouldn't find those two skill sets in the one person. It stands to reason. But here's the thing that gets me, I spent 40 years in a bank—if I'd only known there was such a job as Nipple Tweaker . . .'

And so it went on into the night. We left the table full of good food, good wine and good feeling and we both slept the sleep of the just.

📣 Rach chauffeurs Jules on a connoisseur's tour of the wine country . . .

The next morning, we started our tour of vineyards. Jules drove to the first one but we agreed that I would take over the driving after that as Jules had every intention of being over the limit by ten o'clock in the morning. She turned right at the end of the driveway, drove 50 metres, and turned right again into our first port of call—Sandalyn, which also happened to be holding an olive oil tasting that day. While Jules got technical with the cellarmaster—Have you got any of the '98 left? Is that French oak I detect?—I tried the olive oils and the dessert wines, then wandered into the garden while Jules completed her tasting. From Sandalyn, we went to Warraroong, then Ivanhoe, followed by Brokenwood, Tamburlaine and Scarborough in quick succession. It's a lucky thing Hunter Valley vineyards have such beautiful gardens. While Jules was adding to her wine collection, I spent my time outside smelling the roses—a flower which seems to be *de rigueur* for gardeners of the Lower Hunter. In between rose smellings, I ferried Jules from one vineyard to another. Although getting progressively more pissed, Jules' sense of direction remained unerring, although it is possible, as I suggested, that she has done this route so many times she can do it on automatic pilot.

At one of the vineyards we saw an elaborate wedding taking place.

'Jules, when you get married,' I said, without a hint of irony, 'why don't you have your wedding up here?'

'Good idea, although I should probably go on a date, or even find someone to have sex with before I start making plans for a wedding day.'

'True,' I agreed.

The Hunter Valley is another big tourist destination which could very well have fallen under the influence of 'twee', but its inhabitants seem to have gone to a lot of effort to avoid that fate. They've gone for artistic instead and have employed architects with advanced views. The result is not always successful; in fact, it's sometimes downright hideous. There's one winery in particular that appears to have been built to resemble a very ugly, concrete wine vat, and a holiday resort that looks like a World War II army training camp, presumably not deliberately. Still, the good citizens of the Hunter Valley should be applauded for their determination to avoid twee-ness and we can forgive them one or two ghastly errors in their pursuit of art.

By about midday, I was bored with smelling the roses and criticising the architecture, so we stopped at a winery with a restaurant attached. Jules wanted to get in one more tasting before lunch. The boot of the car was already full and she had started putting her wine boxes onto the back seat.

'Jules, are we going to have room for our luggage?'

'Of course we are,' she said, with the confidence of the utterly toasted. 'There's plenty of room.'

I let it go. We could deal with that one later. Besides, she was already halfway to the cellar door.

'C'mon, Rach, you're going to love this one—they have a dessert wine to die for. Then we can have lunch, and maybe one of their cheeky little chardies. Whaddya think?'

'Sure,' I said. 'Sounds good.'

Rach watches the customers

But Jules didn't hear my answer. She was already inside and seated at the counter in front of a wine list and four tasting glasses. Next to her was a party of people we'd seen at the previous cellar—five women, all of them over 40, one of them at least 110 and all of them having the time of their lives. Jules greeted them with a nod and a 'hello' but she was a woman with serious work to do and she turned her full attention to the lighter whites. I amused myself watching the customers.

At one end of the counter were two couples, touring the district together. I'd spotted these couples before. Not these particular ones, but this particular type. They're young, not long married, maybe in their late twenties or very early thirties. The women are blonde and thin and the men are thickset and hearty. The men wear big baggy shorts down past their knees, sports shirts and Birkenstock sandals. The women wear three quarter pants and pastel twin sets. The couples range together, facing each other like mirrors. The women cling to the men and the men compete over who knows more about the wine they are drinking. Neither knows anything but that's not the point. The point is—who is the more successful couple, me or you? The couple with the slightly prettier wife and the louder, more confident husband wins. The other couple hopes that some of that shining success will rub off—they get to be a premium couple simply by association.

These are the couples who buy four-wheel drives or Saabs, who live in Cremorne with a view to Mosman, or Bondi with a view to Paddington; the husbands are in law or finance and the wives are in interior decoration or catering. I have often wondered if couples like these are truly happy. There's a hell of a lot of pressure on us singlettes to partner up and when I see couples like this I get a sense that they are together just for the reassurance, the mirroring effect. The slightly more successful couple needs the slightly less successful couple to reassure them that they are envied. The slightly less successful couple needs the slightly more successful couple to confer on them the radiance they secretly feel may be missing, despite their having done everything right. What's startling is the number of these mirroring couples drinking their way through the Hunter Valley wine cellars. I suppose being a wine buff is an essential tool in the armoury of the successful Saab-driving husband. Or possibly drinking is the only way out.

I turned my attention to the group standing next to Jules. Here we had women let out of jail for the weekend. There was an air of girlish high spirits about them and they reminded me of very young teenagers on the bus to their first ever youth camp. Mind you, these teenagers were solidly built citizens in comfy jeans and Hush Puppy sandals. That didn't stop the occasional squeal of delighted laughter that always accompanies a risqué joke.

These women were talking up a storm, and now I looked more closely I could see that Jules had joined in, which, in case you hadn't already guessed, is typical Jules. She has an incredible capacity to chat about nothing to complete strangers. She actually seems to enjoy it, well I know she does enjoy it—she tells me so every time I express amazement at this pastime. She says lots of people like gossiping with new friends. Is that true? Why don't I? I sometimes wonder if I'm missing a gene or maybe I'm autistic or something. Anyway, Jules, I could see, was up to the sticky wines and

I was starving so, though I hate to deprive her of pleasure, I had to break up the gang.

'Oh, I *know*,' she was saying to a chirpy, super-wrinkled woman, 'the price you pay in Sydney is absurd . . .'

'Uh, Jules.'

'Have you tried the shiraz? I think this year it's almost as good as the '98, not that *anything* can be as good as their '98. I got six cases and I've never had a better buy . . .'

'Jules, it's lunch time.'

'Oh, right. Rach, this is Helen. The girls are here on a weekend away from their husbands.'

I love it when I'm right.

'Hi Helen. Are you ready to go, J?'

'Sure, hon. Just let me buy a couple of bottles—we'll have them with lunch.'

'Are you two going to the restaurant?' asked Helen.

'We thought we would, yes,' said Jules.

No, Jules! Don't say that, I can see what's coming!

'Why don't you join us?'

Aaargggh.

'Great idea. We'd love to, wouldn't we Rach?'

No. We. Wouldn't.

'Sure,' I lied. 'That'd be lovely.' No, Jules, no, how can you do this to me? I know what it's going to be like. I'm going to have to make meaningless chitchat with people I don't know but I'm sure I won't like. Curses, curses, curses. Jules thinks everyone is wonderful and the chance to meet more people should never be turned down. I keep telling her—there is only a small band of people worth knowing, and we already know them.

However, once you've been suckered in to one of these events, the only thing to do is brace yourself and use the time to practise social skills that would fall into complete disuse if it weren't for friends like Jules. I followed them into the restaurant and tried to pick the woman who looked least chirpy and objectionable, opting in the end for the 110-year-old woman. Perhaps she'd be too deaf or senile to want to chat.

♈ Jules isn't that drunk

Ha ha ha. I knew what Rach was thinking—she's a woman whose every thought and feeling is written on her face— but I shanghaied her into it, partly because I was a bit tiddly and partly because I felt like a party at that point. Helen and her friends had come up on a three-day weekend away from their husbands and they were enjoying themselves hugely. They'd booked themselves into a resort with a golf course and they were golfing in the mornings, wine tasting during the day and partying at night. I thought we might just as well join in the fun. I left Rach to find a soul-mate and, true to form, she chose to sit next to Enid, the oldest and surliest of the group. Enid was there with her daughter, Sal. The other two, I learned upon introduction, were Penelope and Marg. I'd been bonding with Helen, a bright little bird of a woman and a country girl originally. She and her farmer husband had left the land during the drought of '98 and settled in Sydney to be near their grandchildren. Helen did the social thing and drew Rach into the conversation.

'Jules has been telling me about the Holiday Buddy System you two have going. That sounds like a fun idea. How are you enjoying the Hunter Valley?'

'Fine,' said Rach. 'We like it a lot. I don't know that you'd want to be on your own, though.'

'No,' Helen agreed, 'drinking is more of a group activity, isn't it? We're here pretending to be single women. It's Enid's anniversary, so we thought we'd celebrate by leaving her husband to get his own meals for the weekend.'

'How long have you been married, Enid?' I asked.

'Fifty-eight years this Sunday.' She didn't look overjoyed but Rach was on social auto-pilot and offered the appropriate congratulations.

'Wow, 58 years,' she said, summoning up enthusiasm. 'That's amazing. It's a really long time to be with someone. Was is worth it?'

'No,' Enid replied.

Rach was startled, and looked at Enid more closely. 'What?'

'No, it wasn't worth it.'

'But don't you know each other really well? Aren't you completely comfortable in each other's company?' Rach trotted out her conceptions of what marriage would be like.

'Oh, I suppose so. You get used to each other in much the same way as you'd get used to being beaten over the head if it happened often enough.' Enid was uncompromising. 'There should be a statute of limitations on marriage. You should be able to bail out after seven years. Every seven years you get to choose whether to stay or to go.'

Rach was warming to Enid. Here was her ideal role

model—precisely the sort of cranky ancient Rach would like
to be when her time comes, God willing.

I was beginning to think our lunch was going well when
Penelope piped up: 'So what are you girls doing here—are
you escaping from husbands, too?' She'd been engaged in
chat at the other end of the table and had only just come
into the conversation.

'No, we're single. We've come here to add to my wine
collection.'

'Oh, you're not married!' said Penelope, commiserating.
'Do you have children?'

'Er, no,' I said.

'Do you have a pet?' Penelope wanted me to have
something worthwhile in my life.

'Um, no,' I said again.

'Oh,' and she seemed to be at a loss to know what else
to say. What does one say to a pathetic, status-less, singlette
who doesn't even have a pet to call her own?

Rach's face was a study. 'Are *you* married, Penelope?' she
asked, and I recognised that brittle tone. Penelope had only
seconds to live.

'Of course,' she replied. The very idea of not having a
husband was outlandish. 'Roger is away on business. He's
very successful.'

'Is he?' said Rach, sounding like Blackadder just before
he smacks Baldrick on the head. Enid gave a muffled laugh.
Those two were going to become friends, I could tell.

I was tempted to let Rach rip into the patronising
Penelope, but out of habit I came to the social rescue. 'What
does Roger do?' I asked hurriedly.

'He's in the money market,' Penelope said, eyeing Rach defensively, 'and he works very hard. He's a good husband and father. I don't know where I'd be without him.'

'And your pet, Penelope, is it away on important business in Hong Kong?'

Rach said that, you'll be surprised to hear, but I gave her the '*Stop now, love*' look and shook my head slightly, and she sheathed her claws. We long ago agreed that I'd let her know when she needs to lay down her hackles. In return, she lets me know when I'm steamrolling reluctant people into my latest enthusiasm. It's a gift we give each other.

Helen leapt into the breech.

'You have no idea how much I envy you two. Marriage was expected in my day but I don't know that I'd do it again, even with my lovely Jack. And he *is* a lovely man but, oh, how I wish for a bit of space now and then, not to mention a tidy house.'

'Really?' This was a new one on me. 'But what about the security and the company? That's what I'm missing.'

'Exactly,' said Penelope. 'It must be terribly lonely on your own.'

'I suppose I am secure,' mused Helen, 'and we've built a good life together, but when you're a wife and mother you spend your life looking after other people. At first you clean up after little children, then gradually you find you're cleaning up after big children and your husband has decided to join the kids. If the roof fell in, Jack wouldn't notice. He'd just shift down the sofa, keep reading the paper and leave me to deal with it.'

'But it's all worth it for the companionship,' said Penelope stoutly.

Marg, a large comfy woman in her fifties, joined the conversation. 'Pen, exactly how much time do you and Roger spend talking to each other?' Marg sounded like she knew something we didn't.

'We talk all the time!' said Penelope.

'What sort of talk, though? Reminding him of family birthdays and arranging his weekend social calendar doesn't count.'

'Roger's a very busy man,' said Penelope, 'with very important work to do.'

'Mm hmm.' Marg didn't sound convinced. 'What I miss about being single is the freedom. Sometimes I wish I could just decide to—oh I don't know—travel to Turkey, and just drop everything and do it. There'd be no-one to say, "What about me, what am I going to do while you're in Turkey?"'

'The freedom is fun,' said Rach thoughtfully, 'If I want to go away, I just board Thelma and go. And if I need a travel companion, I call Jules.'

'Rach and I have resigned ourselves to single life. We're travel buddies, in the absence of husbands,' I said.

'That's funny,' said Marg. 'I'm married and my husband and I like being together, but I still need travel buddies. Sam won't go anywhere unless there's fishing and I hate fishing. We took the kids on holidays but when they left home we agreed to taking holidays from each other. It works well.'

'Wish I'd thought of doing it earlier,' said Enid, 'Could have saved myself years of miserable holiday time.'

'Oh, Mum, he's not that bad,' said Sal, loyally.

'Really, Enid,' said Penelope sharply, 'you mustn't say things like that in front of your daughter. Besides, Tom has provided well for you.'

'There is the financial aspect,' I added. 'You're definitely poorer if you're single.'

'Right,' agreed Rach, 'unless you marry Ricardo.' She had a point.

'Tom provided for us and in return he got to be as bad-tempered as he likes, whenever he likes,' said Enid. 'He got a house he never had to clean, a garden he never had to tend, and children he never had to talk to. Give me my life back and I'd do it all differently. And Pen, it's no good getting all moral on me. Roger is every bit as horrible and selfish as Tom.'

'I resent that, Enid.' Penelope was close to tears. 'Roger has a lot on his mind. His job is very, very hard.'

'Yes, of course it is,' Helen said. 'Enid, I do wish you'd stop teasing her. Penelope is very happily married, aren't you dear? Very lucky to have a husband like Roger.'

'Very,' said Penelope. 'Roger and I are very happy together.'

I heard Enid mutter to Rach, 'It's the Valium talking,' but fortunately Helen had turned the conversation to golf and Penelope didn't hear this aside. Rach stifled a giggle and for the rest of the lunch Enid regaled her with the tale of her disastrous marriage. Rach came away from that table looking very thoughtful indeed.

CHAPTER ELEVEN

Hey, this ain't so bad

⅄ Why is single so bad?

'How about Penelope and her "Do you have a pet?"' said Rach as we drove away.

'I know. Could you believe that?'

'I've been thinking, Jules, that there is a lot of pressure on single girls to be married. If we didn't have the pressure, do you think we'd be happier being single?'

'What do you mean?'

'I mean we just assume that we have failed somehow if we don't have husbands. I don't know about you, but my parents are eternally disappointed in me. In my family there's my brother, a dentist with a wife and three kids; my sister, a lawyer with a husband and one kid; and me—a poet with ageing eggs and not even the hint of a boyfriend. I'm the black sheep. They don't mind about my failing career, it's my inability to get married that worries them. Every so often my father looks at me and says, "I can't understand it, a pretty girl like you." My mother keeps giving me leaflets for Jewish singles events. Remember when I won the West Wyalong Regional Librarians' Literary Award? I told my aunt and she said, "Did you? Whatever happened to that nice boy you were seeing?" I said, "I won an award, Aunty Lou, it's a really big thing." And she said, "I thought you liked him. When do we see you married?" It's as though I'm not complete until I have a husband. Did I tell you I actually went along to a singles gig?'

'No! I don't believe it!'

'It's true, I did.'

'You didn't! When?'

'About six months ago.'

'You kept that close to your chest. Why didn't you tell me?'

'I don't know,' said Rach, 'I didn't want you to get all excited and think that something may come of it when I knew it wouldn't.'

'Fair enough. But Rach, I'm so impressed. I never in a million years thought you'd go to a singles party. What happened?'

'It was precisely as I'd expected. A complete waste of time.'

The sad story of Swingles

I only went to this party because a friend's mother was hosting it and because people keep on telling me that if I don't get out and meet men I'll stay single forever. The truth of the matter is that I enjoy my quiet life. It's not A-list parties and cocktail franks every night; it's more snuggling into bed at nine thirty with a good book. Pathetic, I know, but very enjoyable and very peaceful. True, having someone around to decipher my superannuation statements would be nice, or to give me a hug when I'm feeling down. But just when I'm thinking along those lines, Thelma cuddles up to me, starts her engine and gives me the look that says 'I adore you'—do you think a man would do that every night like she does? No, nor do I.

Anyway, my friends are right—if I don't get out there I'll just read away the rest of my life. On this particular night, there was an episode of 'Frasier' showing that I hadn't seen before so I had a doubly difficult time dragging myself away from the house, as if my Elizabeth George thriller weren't enough. But I put on the glad rags and drove to an impressively large and expensive house in the Eastern Suburbs, marked out from its neighbours by balloons and fairy lights. This was an official singles party. They'd called it 'Swingles' to give the impression that a bunch of light hearted, happy-go-lucky people were getting together to dance the night away. The entry fee was twenty dollars and you had to register. I gave a fake last name and address, just in case, and received in return a sticker with my name written on it. I had hardly finished signing the book when a very large man who had been hovering near the entrance came charging up to me, stood right over me and in a thick, booming South African accent said, 'My name's Ernest.'

I'm really very polite when I'm forced to socialise, so I didn't duck and run. 'Hi Ernest, my name's Rach.'

'Do you live in the East?' He was bellowing straight into the top of my head.

'Erm, no.'

'Do you live in the North then?'

'No,' I said. 'I live in the West.'

'I've just moved from the North to the East.' This was going to be a tough conversation, I could tell.

'And where did you live when you were in the North?' I asked, sounding interested.

'Gordon,' shouted this huge fellow, still towering over me.

'Really? You surprise me. Most South Africans live in St Ives.'

'Eh?'

'Never mind. Do you enjoy living in the East?'

'Yes.' Long pause. I couldn't think of a thing to say, and neither could he.

'Oh, good. Now, I must just fix up my registration and then say hello to my hostess. Do please excuse me, Ernest, won't you?'

And I made good my escape. Ernest's hunter's eyes followed my progress, so I grasped my hostess's hand, and said, 'Hello Viv, thank you for holding this party. I wonder if you could do something for me?'

'Certainly, my dear.'

'Help me escape from Ernest.'

'Certainly, my dear.' I got the feeling I wasn't the first to make the request.

Viv led me to a couple of people I knew—a friend of mine who sings in the synagogue choir and some mate of hers—and I settled into social mode. It's always nice to know that I can still cut it in the social stakes if I need to. I looked around and saw a poor woman standing on the edge of the party looking miserable and self-conscious, hating every minute and knowing she wasn't going to find a date there, because she was too old ever to date again. I have a rescuer's complex so I went up to her and chatted gently for a bit, but she was too tense to recognise a supporter when she saw one. She was consumed by her own sense of inadequacy, poor thing.

And she wasn't the only one. The worst of singles parties is the air of seething desperation. Some people are there just for the hell of it, and they're okay, happy to chat of this and that and then move on. But some are there to find a partner and the anxiety seeps out of every pore. At this party I twice found myself talking to men in this category and both times I could spot the moment when they thought, 'This is The One.' No, no I am not. I am not The One. You just think I'm The One because we're having a pleasant conversation and you are desperate for this conversation to be the beginning of the end of your search. But try telling them that. One, who was 60 if he was a day, asked me for my number—code for 'Let's date'. I said, thank you but no, and he actually tried to argue the point.

'No, really, give me your number.'

'That's very sweet of you, but I don't think I will,' I said, with admirable patience I think you will agree.

'If you don't get out there and try, how will you ever find a partner?'

'I beg your pardon?' I used my chilly tone.

'What are you looking for in a man?' he asked, unabashed.

'A good listener.'

'You won't find a better listener than me,' he said, 'I have a lot of women friends and they all agree that I'm the best listener they know. It's my profession—I'm a lawyer, so listening is my job. Nine years ago I . . .' And on and on he went. In the end, I simply walked away. As the evening wore on I'd occasionally catch his voice saying, 'What are you looking for in a man?' and I'd rapidly move off in the other direction.

The other odd thing about this party was the number of people who knew each other from the singles scene. I heard this conversation: 'Did you go to the one in Melbourne last week?' 'Yes, Liz was there. I don't think things worked out with her and George.' 'Can't have, George is here and he's in the kitchen with Ellen.' What, I wondered, was the point of coming to a singles party full of people you'd already met and, presumably, rejected? I can confirm that George was in the kitchen with Ellen. They were both very drunk and kissing in a way that reminded me strongly of early teen parties.

I was just thinking of going when Viv, the party's hostess, banged on a glass and called the party to order. It was time to give away the door prize, a bottle of champers, but Viv had a few things she wanted to say first.

'I just want to thank you all for coming and making this party such a success.' There was a round of applause and some shouts of 'Thanks for hosting, Viv.'

'And I know,' continued Viv, 'that if we all stick together . . .' her voice rose to the pitch of a Southern Baptist minister at a spiritual healing, '. . . we can make it through this!'

The party-goers burst into cheers and hugged each other. There were even a few tears. I was appalled. This was like an AA meeting. It was as if being single was a disorder that required social workers, medication and the caring support of other sufferers. I had no idea people were this upset about it. And then the music started and two brave souls began to jiggle about on the dance floor. That was enough for me. I headed towards the door, but found my way blocked in no uncertain terms by a gigantic South African.

'Do you want to dance?' bellowed Ernest, standing two centimetres away from me.

'It's very lovely of you to ask, but I have to go now. Thank you so much for a wonderful evening,' and I did a quick double shuffle, dodged around him and sprinted for the door. Outside, I made a vow—never again.

👓 🍸 Back to the car, and a confession

'I know what you mean,' said Jules. 'I've only been to a few singles parties but there's something about them that isn't entirely healthy. I remember one where I was the youngest person by about twenty years. Not only did no-one speak to me, they wouldn't even look at me. I stayed for half an hour, then left, positively depressed.'

'And I thought my parents were desperate to marry me off. They don't know what "desperate" is.'

'Why don't you tell your parents you're gay?' said Jules. 'That'll stop them trying to marry you off.'

'Oh, please. First of all, it'll stop nothing and, second of all, my mother's early death on my conscience? Just what I need. No, Jules, Enid was telling me that she thinks there's a lot of pressure on people to be partnered up when you could really have a good life if you're single. And . . . there's something else.'

A silence ensued.

'What?' said Jules.

'What?' said Rach.

'What's the something else?'

'Oh.'

Another silence.

'Rach?'

'This is a bit tricky.'

'Go on.'

'You remember last night Janice was telling us about her friend who's decided she can live without sex, so she and her husband aren't going to bother with that bit any more?'

'Yes.'

'Um. I've never really said this before, but me and sex— I can take it or leave it. I'm not really the last of the red hot mamas.' The last bit came out in a rush.

Jules contemplated what she'd just been told. 'Really?'

'Yes. I know you'll find that strange, but it's true. There's another thing that Ricardo and Byron had in common—I didn't have a lot of sex with either of them. We did in the beginning, but after a few months we settled into being more mates. We had sex, but only occasionally.'

'Wow. Didn't that make things difficult in the relationship?'

'Not really. They were both off their faces most of the time, and they didn't seem to mind one way or the other.'

'Huh.' Jules didn't know what to say.

'It's just that, if I'm honest, I'd be perfectly happy never to have sex again—I don't miss it at all. And if I don't want sex and I'm happiest on my own reading, I'm having a hard time coming up with a reason to change anything about my life. Except for my poetry. I'd like to be Poet Laureate.'

'Yes, that would be good.'

'Yes, it would. But many artists don't get recognised in their own lifetime. Other poets work—T S Eliot worked in a bank. So I figure I'm probably destined to be famous after I die. If I'm famous during my life, my work might die out with me. This way my work will live on forever.'

'That's one way of looking at it.'

'Believe me, it's the only way,' said Rach, 'otherwise you'd go mad. Ooh, I hadn't thought of that. Perhaps I *should* go mad. All good artists go mad.'

'No, don't go mad, Rach. Who will come with me on holidays?'

'You're right. I have my responsibilities to you and Thelma and George to think of. Jules, I've decided—I'm not looking for a partner any more. I'm going to live single. I don't want a partner. There. I've said it.'

'What will your parents say?'

'I don't like scenes so I don't propose to tell them.'

'Fair enough. George will be pleased—you'll be living out his ideal society.'

'Ah yes, of course. The Bachelors.'

George and the Society of Bachelors

George has a dream. He thinks the nuclear family is a counter-biological travesty imposed on us by a society desperate to reproduce itself. He says that all our social problems—drugs, alcoholism, homelessness—arise from this obsessive and misconceived worship of the nuclear family as the only possible unit of social life. The breakdown of the family is not a bad thing, in George's view, it is a natural thing. In a sensibly run society, geared for maximum mental and physical wellbeing, there would be no family units. George thinks that the family unit is the root of all misery and evil, which is not really surprising given George's family unit. He comes from a clan of certifiably crazy Hungarians. His parents managed their children's lives using simple, yet highly developed, techniques of hysteria. 'You vat? You vant to get an earring? Of course, you should do vat you vant, vhy should you mind vat I sink? I only brought you into zis vorld. And ven your father sees it and dies of a heart attack and leaves me starving on a vidow's pension, just remember Georgie, *you always do vat you vant.*' Really, his parents explain everything.

In George Taxi's ideal society we would all live the life of suave bachelors. We would live alone with our adored and adoring pets in spacious, elegant apartments or townhouses. None of us would have tedious jobs. We would all work at interesting, unpressured office jobs, where we would engage in intellectually stimulating activities that would leave us refreshed and renewed. Work would start at a leisurely nine am. At twelve-thirty we'd break for a finely prepared meal—vegetarian, as we'd no longer kill animals for food like barbarians—at two pm we would have a light siesta, three pm return to the office, and at five pm we would cease work. We would then leave our offices and repair to one of the many cocktail bars around the city, there to amuse ourselves with our fellow citizens in charming and creative conversation. At this time, we would also choose our partner for the night. Of course, we would all be handsome and well dressed. We would take our chosen partner home (either home will do—both would be equally delightful) and have mutually satisfying sex. We would not share a bed—we would all have our pets to go home to, feed and cuddle up to in the night. The next day, we would do it all again. Which is a nice thought, isn't it?

♆ Jules contemplates her own singleness

George is, of course, as mad as a cut snake, so it suits him to live alone. But how about Rach and sex, eh? It never occurred to me that anyone might live without sex and be happy. She says she just switches off and her body stops thinking about it. I wish mine would, but it won't—of that I'm quite sure. For me, the worst thing about being single is this terrible sex drought. Rach is right in some respects— if people would only stop feeling sorry for me I'd be perfectly happy living alone. I've seen enough bad marriages to know the value of my lovely, safe, quiet little flat where I can be completely myself and do whatever I want. I certainly don't want a partner at any cost, but I would like to have sex. Two years without (apart from the French Farce and he doesn't count) is killing me. I like sex and all that goes with it—the cuddling, the sleeping with another person, the waking up together—I love it all. And I need it. And I'm getting tired of doing without it.

Okay, so what's missing from my life? Is it just sex? Is that all I need—a lover? Because if that's all I need, I have another complaint—where, just out of interest, are all the red-blooded males? Unlike Rach, I am not buried in my living room. I get out there, I party, I go to pubs, I belong to *three* social clubs, for chrissakes. Three! What do I have to do to meet a man who (a) I want to have sex with and (b) would like to have sex with me? Has the world gone mad? It never used to be this difficult. I'm not even very picky—as long as he's reasonably good looking, has decent social skills and washes regularly, I'm in. I'd be perfectly happy with the life I have now and a lover I could call on whenever I felt the urge.

If I had a lover instead of a partner, then I could kiss goodbye to kids, so my next question is: Will I miss not having children? As I ask myself this, I realise that it's a long time since I thought of motherhood. I'm an aunt a few times over so I have a lot to do with my sister's kids, but my own kids? Now that I've got access to little ones and have seen first-hand what bringing them up involves, I'm pretty sure I can live without them. Do I really want to swap a good career in the public service and freedom to travel for a life of minutiae, sewing on labels, ferrying the kids to ballet and soccer on the weekend, and worrying about whether or not to send them to a Catholic school? My nieces and nephews look on me as an alternative parent, so I'll even get a taste of teenage angst when they decide to run away from home and come to live with me until they realise I'm even tougher than their mum. If I didn't have kids, what, realistically, would I miss? Only cleaning up vomit and spending a fortune on orthodontic work, I should think.

I'll have to give this more thought, but I wonder if Rach isn't right. If the whole world weren't looking at me pityingly, would I still want a husband and kids? I'm pretty sure a long-term fling would do just as well.

Back at the bed & breakfast

We spent a second night at the B&B and left for our final destination, Terrigal, the next morning. We were supposed to leave early, but we hit a snag as we were loading the car. Jules put the wine in first so that it would have a stable surface. All the other luggage was to be fitted around the wine boxes in order to keep them steady during the trip and to protect them on the off chance that we have another accident.

'We'll have to stick to the major highways, I'm afraid,' she said. 'I don't want to take any risks until I've got it all safely stored in my cellar.'

'No problem.' Rach picked up the next box. 'Is there much more, Jules?'

'Just the Sandalyn stickies, the Warraroong malbec and

the Scarborough chardies,' she said, 'Oh, and the ports. Is that what you've got there?'

Rach staggered to the car under about a hundredweight of the Hunter Valley's finest. 'I don't know. The box is so big it's blocking out the sun and I can no longer see. Jules? Jules? Where are you?'

'Very funny.' Jules surveyed the car's interior, 'Hmmm. It'll have to go on the back seat.'

Rach heaved it in and noticed that the floor of the car's rear section was already stacked with wine boxes.

'Erm, Jules, is there going to be enough room to fit everything in?'

'There's only two more boxes.'

'No, I meant our luggage.'

Pause.

'Ah.'

Unusually for the Queen of Organisation, she had become so absorbed in getting her wine just so, she had forgotten about the little matter of our travelling cases—which just shows you how important her cellar is to her.

'Ah,' she said again, and then, 'Ah.'

'I've got an idea,' said Rach, 'why don't we freight all these boxes home?'

'*Post my wine?*'

'Not a good idea? But surely the postal service must ship wine all the time.'

'*Post my wine?*'

'Right, I see. Think again then,' said Rach, getting the picture.

'We are not going to post the wine home,' said Jules, 'but we will have to post something home.'

She looked at our luggage. 'We can mail the camping gear. That's hardy.'

'What? Are you mad? Consign my best tent and sleeping bags to the care of Australia Post? No, no and no. I'd get it back with half the pegs missing and holes in the fly.'

'Oh, I see, the wine can go, but the camping gear's too precious?'

'Jules, let's not send either back. Surely one or two of these suitcases can go? What's in this one, for instance. I don't think we've even opened it.'

'Ski gear.'

'Ski gear? It's September.'

'I know, but I thought there was a chance of a late snowfall at Mount Hotham. And if there was, then we might want to ski, so I brought along the things we'd need—thick socks, ski jackets, mittens. You know.'

'Skis?'

'Well, obviously not skis—we can hire skis. I'm not completely mad.'

'A highly debatable point, some might say.'

'Not if they want to get home in one piece, they wouldn't.'

Rach grinned. 'Let's freight home these two cases then. We still won't fit everything in.'

'Roof racks,' said Jules, 'that's what we need. We'll carry the rest on the roof.'

So we went into town and had roof racks fitted to Jules' car. By the time we piled the rest of our cases on the top of the car, it was midday and our car looked like the one the Clampetts drove in the 'Beverley Hillbillies', or possibly the Griswalds on their European vacation. Not the most debonair look and we'd have to drive at a sedate pace, but we were nearing the end of our trip, so we decided we could live with it. We waved goodbye to Bob and Janice and turned right out of their driveway. Three minutes later, we passed their bed & breakfast again, going the right way this time, and if you'd looked closely you'd have seen two women with their mouths wide open and their fingers moving in precise synchronicity.

CHAPTER TWELVE

We like life after all

Rach and luxury

We'd come to stay at the Crowne Plaza in Terrigal, a well-known destination for Sydney women who want to get away from it all for a weekend of luxury. Jules is very big on luxury holidays but I can't say they do much for me, being more of a camping, nature-loving type. Jules, however, likes to be pampered. She likes the whole steam room, facial, Japanese-woman-walking-on-your-back experience. She likes to sit in spas drinking a glass of crisp chardy and gossiping with the gals. Her idea of a good time is a three-hour telephone conversation. My idea of a good phone call is one the answering machine takes. I don't know how she puts up with me. If I happen to pick up for Jules and she launches into a lengthy description of her weekend, which she usually does, I have to admit that after about ten minutes I switch off and just let my unconscious say, 'Uh huh . . . good idea . . .

sounds great . . . ' whenever her tone seems to require it. Sometimes my unconscious will let me down, the cheeky beggar, and I'll say, 'Super!' just has Jules has told me that her date turned out to be a dud. And sometimes I suspect she deliberately tells me those things in a chirpy voice, just to catch me napping.

I have to say though, that the Crowne Plaza was pretty special. It was a far cry from the motel we stayed at in Canberra where the two of us squished into a room marginally bigger than my bathroom and tried not to fall out of our narrow single beds in the night. This one was luxury with a capital L and even I felt an atavistic yearning to lie back in a pool of bubbles and guzzle champagne. We had two giant double beds, a huge room, a view of the sea, a lovely old bathroom—as you know, I do appreciate a good bathroom. Ooh, and once more we had the joy of telly in bed. This one was a promisingly large telly with not one, but two remote controls—a his and hers. Isn't that gorgeous?

Jules was keen to get out and see the town, so I stopped gazing at the bathroom and playing with the remote controls and we set out on an exploratory tour of the locale.

🍸 Jules on Terrigal

What can I say? I loved this place. I booked myself in for a facial, a shiatsu massage and a pedicure. Rach balked at the prices, which were a bit on the steep side, but I'm as bad as a habitual gambler when it comes to sins of the flesh, so I flexed the credit card and prepared to enjoy. Rach said she thought she'd be fine with the steam room, sauna and spa. She gets toey when she thinks we're being gouged, which I was, but when I was looking and feeling a million dollars I knew I wouldn't care. That was for the afternoon. Meanwhile, in Terrigal itself, the beach was beautiful and the shopping was fantastic—was there anything you couldn't get up here? I bought sunnies, swimmers, a hat, a sarong and two pairs of sandals. The shopping, the beach, the spa, the pool, the massages, the shopping, the people, the chatting— I loved this place! Did I mention the shopping?

👓 Rach on Terrigal

What, are you kidding me? Outside the one flash hotel, this place was a dump. It was Double Bay in a parking lot. Who thought of building a tarmacked car park right on the beach? And where were the trees? There's no point to a beach if it's sea and sand flanked by highway. You need trees, preferably palm trees, to shelter you from the sun and from cars. Beaches should be secluded, surrounded by rocks and dunes and vegetation. They should not be right next to the car park and just across the road from the Manolo Blahnik outlet. Australia is chocker with beaches straight from paradise, and Terrigal is a beach holiday mecca? I'm gobsmacked. And as for shopping, if I wanted to pay three times ordinary retail for a sun hat, I could do that in any eastern suburb of Sydney. ·

'People come here for the resort, Rach.'

'And stay by the pool, I notice. I see no-one's actually on the beach. And who can blame them?'

Mercifully, Jules' appointments with the hotel's beauticians kept her shopping expedition down to about two hours. When we got back to the hotel, she headed for the masseurs and I headed for the pool. We met up again in time for cocktails at the hotel bar.

🍸 One of us gets smashed. No prizes for guessing which one—Me!

Rach lacks the shopping gene, which is why she didn't really appreciate Terrigal as she ought. I found a couple of bargains, but she'd got it into her head that the place was a rip off and nothing, not even the most divine pair of Gucci imitation sunglasses at twenty dollars, yes twenty dollars and looking just like the real thing, would change her mind. But she had a good time in the spa and I, of course, was as high as a kite on massages and expensive moisturisers, so we hit the hotel bar in very high spirits indeed. Who needs drugs when you can feel like this? Ooh, mango daiquiris, my favourite.

The bar was huge and plush with big comfy chairs, a view of the sea, and gorgeous young bartenders, who must have the best job in town—helping unattached women who are looking for fun, adventure and a break from their humdrum lives get very drunk and have a good time. They were so very young, though, really no more than twenty, that I found myself thinking, Surely that would border on the illegal?

Rach and I were there to have a celebratory last night of our holiday. We planned on wrapping ourselves around a few daiquiris, reviewing our holiday, and making resolutions for our return to normal life. We'd started talking that one over on the way down to the bar: Rach's resolution was to ignore pressures on her to get married; mine was to go on a decent first date. We figured these two small adjustments would make us perfectly happy with the single life we had.

Rach wanted to spend some quality time with me and I'd made a commitment to myself not to abandon her to strangers. She'd been very good about that during the last couple of weeks, she'd hardly complained at all as I dragged her around making her talk to people she didn't know, so I owed her an evening with just the two of us. But when we walked into the bar Rach looked around and said, 'See the woman in the orange top in the corner?' I did. 'I was talking to her in the sauna this afternoon. Come and meet her—you'll like her.'

I stopped dead. 'What?'

'Orange Top—I know her.'

'No, I mean, do my ears deceive me? *You* chatted to a stranger in a sauna?' I can't recall the last time we met new people through Rach. Oh, yes I can. Never. Rach even seemed pleased to see her. I looked wonderingly at this Rach I'd never seen before. She caught my eye and grinned, 'Shut up, you. I'm not a complete social wreck.'

Orange Top seemed equally pleased to see Rach, and hailed her like an old friend—Rach must have been in good form in the sauna. On closer inspection, we saw that she was not alone. She was sitting next to a man who was at that moment engaged in writing on a coaster. Rach performed the introductions—Orange Top's name was Jennifer—and Jennifer turned to the man sitting next to her saying, 'This is a friend of mine, Steve.'

Steve looked up, looked straight into my eyes and gave me one of the most blinding smiles it's ever been my privilege to see. He was a man with that slightly rumpled look I do so love: teeth slightly crooked, smile slightly askew, hair just a little tousled, a bit like a rumpled George Clooney, only nicer than George—utterly gorgeous, in other words. Momentarily I stopped breathing and took stock: no wedding ring, introduced as 'a friend of mine', which is code for 'nothing to do with me, ladies, the field is clear', no other woman in sight. Tick, tick, tick. I wonder?

'Hi,' said Steve, 'can I get you ladies a drink?' I started breathing again. No, there was just enough lisp there to let me know that Steve was not batting on my team. Oh well, maybe after a few daiquiris the bartenders wouldn't look so young, although I'd probably have to knock Steve out of the way to get to them. I saw Jennifer give Steve an odd look, but I couldn't see that he'd done anything unusual, so I thought no more of it. He went to the bar to order our first round of daiquiris and I settled in for a night of fun.

They were a delight, Jennifer and Steve. They were old friends here on a weekend's shopping and sitting by the pool. Does it surprise you to hear that Steve was a shopaholic? Unlike Rach, he thought my sunnies were the find of the century. We found out Jennifer and Steve were single too, so one thing led to another and soon we were talking about our worst dates ever, annoying 'couple' behaviour (should I ever get a partner, Rach, remind me not to hold hands when we're in company), and sad-eyed relatives. From there, it was a small step to the vexed question of life without sex and Steve and I engaged in the kind of discussion you can only have with a close girlfriend or a gay guy—we talked about one-night stands, lovers and the perils of marriage. We agreed that if we could only find a decent lover with no odd behaviour who'd shag us regularly we'd be happy. We had a marvellous time.

Steve had just returned with our fourth round of daiquiris when we heard the first notes of Gloria Gaynor's 'I Will Survive' on the dance floor. He almost dropped the drinks on the carpet, he was so excited.

'Come on Jules, it's "I Will Survive"! We gotta dance to this one,' and he grabbed me by the hand and pulled me off my chair. I took a backward glance at Rach to make sure she was okay to be left alone, but she and Jennifer were deep in discussion, so I stopped worrying and started dancing. Steve and I boogied up a storm. After Gloria, the DJ played 'YMCA' and of course we both knew all the moves, then 'I Heard It On The Grapevine' then ooh, ooh, ooh, ABBA—Steve had sound views on ABBA too. Why, oh why, are the good ones always gay? I'm not asking for much but I would like to have sex just one more time before I die, and Steve would be my perfect candidate for a lover. Sigh.

At one point I remember Rach coming up to me on the dance floor to say she was turning in—she wanted to watch telly in bed and read. I gave her a kiss goodnight and saw her to the door, getting another round on my way back. Some time later, Jennifer also retired and Steve and I were left to party on. I don't recall much more—I can remember standing outside chatting and having an illicit cig, I can remember dancing a lot, and I can remember Steve and I had to lean on each other just to make it up the stairs to bed. I vaguely recall Rach snoring loud enough to rattle the windows and thinking that I really must get some ear plugs from the local chemist, but that's the last thought I can remember. I must have crashed as soon as my head hit the pillow.

Breakfast—and one last diatribe from Rach

Call me picky, but when I pay a fortune to stay in a hotel which bills itself as five star, I expect five star all the way. The most irritating thing happened this morning. Our deal included breakfast, which I had on my own, Jules still being unconscious. She must have had a blast last night. I didn't even hear her come in, it was so late. Anyway, breakfast was in the dining room, and they claim to make eggs for you on the spot, exactly as you like them. I was determined to experience this. I love eggs and the worst thing about travelling is having to eat poached eggs with rock hard yolks or watery scrambled eggs on barely toasted toast. The dining room at this hotel still makes you cook toast on that ridiculous rolling toaster which takes four hours to slightly brown one side of the bread, then you have to do it all again. There was, however, a young man at a cart making, as advertised, eggs to order. I made my calculations and decided to cook the toast first, and put up with cold toast for the sake of hot and excellent fried eggs.

Toast on plate, I went up to the cart and waited while two women in front of me ordered omelettes, which he did indeed make to perfection. My turn came. Now, I am very particular about my eggs: I like fried, whites hard, yolks soft. I said this to him. He agreed that he could make them just like that. He picked up an egg, cracked it, it fell in the pan. He picked up the second egg. Cracked it, it fell in the pan. And broke. Here's the bit I'm fuming about—he didn't ditch it and make another. I couldn't believe it. If I want a broken fried egg I can do that myself, I don't need to pay a king's ransom in room tariff to have someone do it for me. And here's the bit I'm fuming about even more—I didn't say a word. I just fumed silently. And then, when he gave them to me and said, 'All right?' I just looked at him. I did not say, 'Of course it's not all right—is that a perfect egg? No! It's broken. Do it again.' I just took them away and fumed.

I tried to tell Jules about the eggs on my return to our room, but she waved me silent, incapable of speech herself and needing only silence. I saw the condition she was in and considerately restrained myself. Her burdens were heavier than mine just then. I could always tell her when we got back to Sydney.

ᐯ 𝖸 Jules and Rach call home

We agreed that Rach should drive the last leg home as Jules was having trouble seeing. She was too delicate for our usual spirited rendition of 'Dancing Queen', and we drove for some time in companionable silence until Jules broke the unaccustomed quiet.

'Rach, do you think I should become Australia's first Bachelorette?'

'What's that?'

Rach doesn't watch enough television.

'It's the female equivalent of "The Bachelor"—the guy on TV who got to choose a girlfriend out of 25 blond bombshells. If I were Australia's Bachelorette, I'd have 25 gorgeous hunks vying to be my husband.'

'Really? Are they on the level?'

'Yep.'

'Isn't it staged for TV, like the wrestling?'

'No, of course not.'

'I bet it is. If they were all hunks, they'd have to be gay.'

'They'd be from all over Australia, not just Sydney.'

'Then all I have to say is, "You go, girl!"'

Jules lapsed into silence once more to contemplate the likelihood of her Bachelor dream boys being gay.

'Why are all the good ones gay, Rach? Tell me that. Look at Steve.'

'Steve?'

'The guy we met last night. Now *there's* a spunk. Charming, handsome, funny, smart, likes mango daiquiris— is there nothing wrong with this guy? Ooh, only his unavailability to me.'

'What makes you think he's gay?'

'Oh, come on, Rach. One, he can dance—I rest my case right there; but if you're still not convinced, then: two, his mannerisms—screaming queen; three, he knows all the words to "Dancing Queen"; four, he has great dress sense and he told me he liked my shoes; five, he's a hairdresser; and six, I don't need more than those five, because that says it all. Tell me that guy isn't gay.'

'That guy isn't gay.'

'What are you talking about? You didn't even spend any time with him.'

'And yet, I know that that guy isn't gay.'

'Oh yeah, how?'

'Jennifer told me. Get this: we were talking about gay men, and how it's so much easier getting to know a gay guy than it is getting to know a straight guy. She told me that Steve has a ploy. Whenever he meets a girl he likes, he gets instantly nervous she won't like him if she thinks he's hitting on her, so he pretends to be gay. That way, she talks to him, dances with him, hugs him . . . Did you hug him, Jules?'

'Did I?! I was tanked on mango daiquiris and he was cute as! What do you think? I hugged him, I danced with him, he practically carried me all the way back upstairs. If I'd known he was straight, I'd have slept with him.'

'She says he gets heaps of women that way. Did he ask for your number?'

Pause.

'Yes. Yes, he did.'

'Ooh, ooh, turn on your mobile. I bet he's messaged you.'

She did.

Bleep Bleep.

'Is it him? What does it say?'

'Good Lord. It *is* him. He wants to know if I want to

catch up in Sydney for a drink. You know what this means, don't you Rach?'

'I do indeed, Jules.' And together we cried, 'The drought is broken!'

'Where's your mobile, Rach?'

'It's in the glove box. Why?'

'I'll check your messages for you.'

'Must you? I want to stay on holiday.' But it was too late. Jules can't resist a mobile, and the prospect of sex had perked her right up and out of her hangover.

Bleep Bleep.

'Bugger. Who is it?'

'There are eight of them.'

'*Eight!* I don't know eight people, do I?'

'They're all from George Taxi.'

'George messaged me eight times? What does he say?'

'I'll read them out,' said Jules.

Picked up Thelma. She fine. Have good hol. xxx G.

Thelma misses u. Crying and looking wan. Will feed her sashimi. Hope all well. xxx G.

Thelma under couch. Won't come out. Kitty stalking her. What is favourite toy? Will try that. Enjoy selves. x G.

Thelma whining. Does this whining never stop? Still under couch. WHAT IS FAVOURITE TOY? Pls reply. G.

What stops Thelma whining?? Immediate reply required. G.

Where fuck r u? Why fuck not answer messages??

Thelma out from under couch. Peed in Kitty's feed bowl. I blame her upbringing.

If don't get home soon, Kitty will tear Thelma new bunghole and long friendship b/w self and u will come to crashing halt. CAN'T TAKE ANY MORE OF THIS!

'Sounds like the girls didn't get on too well at Uncle George's place,' said Jules.

'That's not Thelma's fault. Kitty is psychotic. Poor Thelma must think I've abandoned her to a nut house.'

'George will have been hand feeding her the finest sashimi known to mankind, so she just might think the nut house is preferable to you and Whiskas.'

'With Kitty in the nut house? I think not,' said Rach. 'Still, best pick her up ASAP, before the two of them send George to the men in white coats. Poor George, just what he doesn't need—another demanding, crying, impossible-to-please female in his life.'

🍸 The last story

'Rach, can we go to the Korean Bath House before we pick up Thelma? I'm not quite ready to end our holiday. I feel so good, I just want to have one more outing.'

'I know what you mean. Okay. I might even splurge and

have a massage—I'll need one if I'm going to face the wounded glare of a betrayed cat.'

So we took one final indulgent trip. We went to the Korean Bath House in Kings Cross. We sauna-ed, we spa-ed; we washed our hair and bodies clean; we plunged ourselves into the freezing pool, then the hot pool, then the ginseng pool; strong-fingered Korean women massaged every last knot out of our shoulders. Finally, we wrapped ourselves in fluffy white bathrobes and went into the relaxation room to down a couple of crisp whites.

Leaning back into the chairs, our skin glowing with expensive moisturiser, our bodies relaxed, Jules said, 'We're right back where we started Rach—remember the fluffy white bathrobes at the health retreat?'

'We didn't need to go away at all,' said Rach. 'We could have stayed right here and had the perfect holiday.'

'But then we'd have missed out on singing 'Dancing Queen' while doing 110 down the freeway.'

'How true,' said Rach, and we both started quietly singing our anthem: '*You* can dance! *You* can ji-ive! *Having* the time of your li-i-ife . . .' and our finger movements began of themselves.

'Life is good, Rach.'

'That it is, Jules.'

'More chardy, Rach?'

'Don't mind if I do, Jules.'

Acknowledgements

The authors wish to thank the following people for their valuable contributions: Jessica Block, Leonie Cambage, Lisa Campton, Anne Fitzsimmons, Steve Foyle, Peter Godfrey-Smith, Ray Gordon, Zina Gorelick Weiss, Danielle Grant, Basma Greiss, Julie Gustavs, Paula Hannagan, Dean Johns, Cynthia Kardell, Alwyn Karpin, Angela Karpin, Barbara Lasserre, George Madarasz, Bob Oxenbould, Janice Oxenbould, Rachel Petro, Tyrone Pitsis, Ruth Rack, Thelma Weiss, Zdenek Weiss.